salmonpoetry

Diverse Voices from Ireland and the World

LELAND BARDWELL 1922-2016

Photo: Bobbie Hanvey

Born in India, to Mary (née Collis) and William Patrick Hone (known as Pat), Leland Bardwell grew up in Leixlip, County Kildare. She was educated at Alexandra School and later at the University of London. Living at times in Paris, London, Scotland, Kilkenny, Dublin and Monaghan, she settled in Sligo in 1991.

From adolescence until the 1970s her life was turbulent, she immersed herself in literary and artistic circles in Soho, London, and Dublin, befriending such figures as Robert MacBryde and Robert Colquhuon, Patrick Kavanagh, and in Dublin, John Jordan, Eiléan Ní Chuilleanáin, Macdara Woods, Pearse Hutchinson, Michael Hartnett, James Liddy, Hayden Murphy, Paul Durcan, Neil Jordan and many others involved in poetry, prose and theatre.

Embracing a very unconventional approach to life, she had seven children by a number of different men. She married once, to Michael Bardwell. She brought to her poetry, plays and prose a clear and unsentimental empathy for those marginalised by their gender, poverty, lack of education or emotional injuries, and the work was informed by the life without being self-regarding.

As well as the five collections of poetry included in this volume, she published five novels, a book of short stories, a memoir, and had four stage plays and a number of radio plays produced. Unpublished work includes more stories and a novella, published in 2022 by Doire Press, six other plays never produced, a TV film adaptation, a feature film script based on the hiring fairs, and a libretto written for Siobhán Cleary's opera, *Jack Ashore*.

Her prose and poetry was translated into German, Polish, Spanish, French, Albanian and Turkish.

Leland Bardwell was active in publishing: a co-founder of *Cyphers*, one of the longest running poetry magazines in the world, she also was a member of the Irish Writers' Co-operative in the mid 1970s, and was centrally involved in the Scríobh Literary Festival in the 1990s-2000s. She was a founding member of Aosdána, Ireland's state-sponsored academy for creative artists.

Leland Bardwell's Publications & Productions

POETRY

The Mad Cyclist (New Writers' Press, 1970)
The Fly and the Bedbug (Beaver Row Press, 1984)
Dostoevsky's Grave: Selected Poems (The Dedalus Press, 1991)
The White Beach: New and Selected Poems, 1960-1998 (Salmon Poetry, 1998)
The Noise of Masonry Settling (Dedalus Press, 2006)
Them's Your Mammy's Pills and other poems (Dedalus Press, 2015)

NOVELS

Girl on a Bicycle (The Irish Writers Co-operative, 1977,
also Liberties Press 2009 & 2014)
That London Winter (Irish Writers' Co-op Books, 1981)
The House (Brandon, 1984, reissue Blackstaff Press 2006),
also as *Das Haus* (Parthas Verlag, 2007)
There We Have Been (Attic Press, 1989)
Mother to A Stranger (Blackstaff Press, 2002).
Also as *Mutter Eines Fremden* (Diana Verlag, 2005)

SHORT STORIES

Different Kinds of Love (Attic Press, 1987 reissue Dedalus Press, 2012,
also as *Zeit Vertreibt Liebe* (Ullstein Taschenbuch 1991 and 1998)
The Heart and The Arrow (Doire Press, 2022)

MEMOIR

A Restless Life (Liberties Press, 2008)

STAGE PLAYS

Thursday (Players Theatre, TCD, 1974)
Open-ended Prescription (The Peacock Theatre, 1979)
No Regrets (Gorey Arts Festival Commission 1984,
staged in Gorey and the National Stadium, Dublin)
Jocasta (2001) *Dhá Ean* (Sligo) and the Belltable Arts Centre (Limerick)

RADIO PLAYS

The Revenge of Constance
Just Another Killing
The Happy Birthday (RTE)
Open Ended Prescription, radio version (BBC broadcast 3rd Sept, 1979)
Quiet Waters (BBC, 1980)

Leland Bardwell

Collected Poems

EDITED BY
JOHN MCLACHLAN

salmonpoetry

Published in 2022 by
Salmon Poetry
Cliffs of Moher, County Clare, Ireland
Website: www.salmonpoetry.com
Email: info@salmonpoetry.com

ISBN 978-1-915022-17-2

Cover Painting by Janet Pierce
www.janetpierce.com

Cover Design & Typesetting: *Siobhán Hutson*

Printed in Ireland by Sprint Print

Salmon Poetry gratefully acknowledges the support of
The Arts Council / An Chomhairle Ealaíon

I want to take the hand of the past
as round and clean as an autumn apple

and hold it tight as a nail
till all the talking is done

Acknowledgements

Salmon Poetry would like to thank the rights holders of publications in which some of the poems in this volume first appeared, in particular New Writers' Press, Beaver Row Press and Dedalus Press for allowing us to reproduce poems from collections they have previously published.

The editor of this volume would like to thank Jessie Lendennie of Salmon Poetry in particular for agreeing to publish it.

Thanks also to those who assisted in the hunt for poems in periodicals during trying times: Eiléan Ní Chuilleanáin for many trips to TCD library and the National Library of Ireland, Eamon Carr, Gerald Mangan, Tom Hadden, Geraldine O'Reilly, Anna-Maria Arwanitaki, Laura Loftus, Peter Fallon and Alan Hayes for sending copies of poems via email.

Thanks to Nicholas McLachlan for assistance and encouragement.

Contents

The Poems

*

Poems in Periodicals & from Bardwell's Papers, 1960s

*

from *The White Beach*
(Salmon Poetry, 1998: Sixties)

*

The Mad Cyclist
(New Writers' Press, 1970)

*

Poems in Periodicals & from Bardwell's Papers, early 1970s

*

from *The White Beach* (Salmon Poetry, 1998: Seventies)

*

Poems in Periodicals & from Bardwell's Papers

*

The Fly and the Bedbug

(Beaver Row Press, 1984)

*

Poems in Periodicals & from Bardwell's Papers

*

from *The White Beach*
(Salmon Poetry, 1998: Eighties)

*

Dostoevsky's Grave
(Dedalus Press, 1991)

*

Poems in Periodicals & from Bardwell's Papers

*

from *The White Beach*
(Salmon Poetry, 1998: Nineties)

*

Poems in Periodicals & from Bardwell's Papers

*

The Noise of Masonry Settling
(Dedalus Press, 2006)

*

Poems in Periodicals & from Bardwell's Papers, 2000s

*

Other early poems

INTRODUCTION

by

Eiléan Ní Chuilleanáin

Everyone who knew Leland Bardwell remembers her outstanding qualities: of energy, generosity and tolerance. Readers of her partial autobiography, *A Restless Life*, will have got a sense of her character, along with her humour, her literary skill and her determination not to look away from the truth of her own experience. Those who knew her well were conscious of an intellectual rigour and firmness, something that might not have been so evident in the chaotic encounters where she so often found herself.

Now that her poems, here collected in their entirety, are available to readers, her long-time admirers will recognise the writer they knew, but will also be able to see how she developed as a poet. There are reasons why this has been difficult until now. Like many poets she began by publishing in magazines, and the work did not always reappear in book form, although she published five collections. Some did make it into a book, but years after their first appearance—and there is evidence that she had been revising them in the meantime. The editor has set out to give the poems in chronological order of composition, though it has not always been possible to be certain.

What her revisions and exclusions show is how serious she was about the form and texture of her poems. The reader senses always that among the elements that go into the making of her poems there is that preliminary gauging of perspective that leads to the decision that in this case a poem is what must emerge—after all, she wrote plays, short stories and novels as well. In her poems there is often an element of fiction, but the dominant chord is truth, the ways in which language points towards truth even from the angle of invention. And while the poems that survive began to appear when she was in her forties, we can see her growing as a poet, particularly growing in confidence and the ability to assert a unique personal point of view.

Patrick Kavanagh, her friend and guest, who encouraged her to write poetry, had written what he hoped might be said about himself, 'He knew that posterity has no use/ for anything but the soul,/ the lines that speak the passionate heart/ the spirit that lives alone.' Of all her contemporaries she is the one who most took his attitude to heart, though like him she gives form its due importance. And like his, her spirit may live alone, surely unique, but it's a spirit that goes in quest of human beings. We may remember that Kavanagh also wrote, addressing 'Irish poets', that 'Even Cabra may surprise'.

She finds surprises in Camden Street, in Pimlico, in the Iveagh Hostel, in Mountjoy Prison. The poems reflect her lively engagement with people, often those near the margins of society, who still refused to be brushed aside: the street stallholder who shared whiskey at Christmas and maternal solidarity, and when the moment came to die, called a taxi to carry her off from her pitch; or the woman who went on strike against the early closing hour in the Iveagh hostel because she preferred to stay in the pub. The mental patient who absconds in the confusion set loose when he lets a bird out of its cage; the prisoner serving forty years. Recognisable as well is the instant suspicion of authority: claimed by professionals (solicitors 'sit/ tearing the hospital cloth/ with their ravenous backsides') prison officers, landlords.

Her own story, with its moments of hilarity and its questioning of the past, sometimes produces a guilt that demands to be explored, sometimes a clearsighted defiance,

> My children, I said, romp away
> this little strip is yours
> for the dead are mostly idle
> and do not care if you are naked
> naked from the waist down.

The coalface of motherhood as she experienced it. And her labouring relationship with her own mother, never finally dealt with, but eloquently expressed in the late 'Seal sequence'.

When she read poems by others it was inauthenticity that she reacted against most—as co-editor of *Cyphers* I often saw how fast she was to sniff it out. None of this means that she didn't care about technique; she loved to discover a poem that was sharply written, interesting and surprising. Her own poems usually do not draw attention to their form, though there is the occasional resounding conclusion:

Your daddy's gone but what is worse
I wish that I had left him first. ('Lullaby')

It happens more often that the voice is deceptively relaxed:

For they shall return whence they came
like landlords who get no rent.
But we promised we'd pay the rent
and we believed it. But we didn't do it.

So that's why they kept coming back.
('They Put a Bed in the Passage')

I can't resist quoting yet another conclusion, to 'The Lady who went on Strike':

... but at least they were able to stop the funeral cortege
from proceeding up Werburgh Street.

This last observation depends on topography and irony. Every poet has to be read in the context of their time, language and place, and a hundred years after her birth it may be time to look at the historical moment that produced her. She was born into an Irish Protestant (*not*, she insisted, 'Anglo-Irish') family which belonged to that Protestant professional class which was not displaced by Irish independence, though it was not treated generously by the new Free State. Unlike the landowning families, the writers, artists, engineers, doctors and lawyers of her family continued to belong to Ireland, to work (and to earn), and their cultural presence was important. Her parents Pat Hone and Mary Collis both came from families with notable literary and artistic impact in their time. Connections included the biographer Joseph Hone (1882-1959), the landscape artist Nathaniel Hone the younger (1831-1917), and the stained-glass artist Evie Hone (1894-1955), and on the Collis side the three writer brothers Maurice, Bob and John Stewart Collis—all of whose entries in the *Dictionary of Irish Biography* are dotted with 'q.v.'s underlining the networks that originated and supported them.

Her childhood was not easy; the third child, the second girl, she felt her parents preferred the other children, and her writings celebrate treasured moments of rebellion: 'my sister and I pissed in the pie-dishes/ on my sixth birthday/ ... It was my idea.' ('Childhood reminder') *A Restless Life* details the stresses of family life, the uneven and then interrupted education, the unhappy relationship especially with her mother, the awkward identity of the Protestant girl, and the series of partly deliberate, partly random events that found her, in her twenties and thirties, a vagrant who has landed as a divorced mother of three children living in London. She frequents the bohemian world of poets and artists, moving back and forth between the liberation and stimulation they offer her and the needs of children whom she feels she neglects but succeeds in caring for. This phase culminates with the beginning of her relationship with the Irish father of her three youngest children and their move back to Ireland.

She came to serious writing, it seems, in the 1960s after her return to Dublin at the start of the decade. I hesitated to make this statement as frequent changes of place, moving between Ireland and Britain up to then, may have involved the loss of earlier work. She was certainly writing from a young age. A poem was published in the *Kilkenny People* around 1950—on, she says, the same day as the report of her arrest for being drunk in charge of a car; she describes the poem as 'terrible.' She had sent a story to *The Bell* just before it ceased publication. But in Dublin she does, finally, emerge. Patrick Kavanagh, whom she had known already in London, as a friend of Katherine Moloney whom he was to marry, enjoyed a particular kind of half-derisive Dublin celebrity. He was recognised as a great poet and he was constantly visible. He had no comfortable, permanent home to retreat to, and her friendship, her growing family of children, gave him respite.

She became part of his literary circle, which included James Liddy, the eminence or impetus or inspiration behind a succession of literary journals, from *Arena* (1963-5), *The Holy Door* (1965-6), *The Lace Curtain* (1969-78) and the later *Gorey Detail* (1977-83), to some more exotic titles, *Nine Queen Bees* (1970), *The Pleiades will weep over Douglas Hyde* (1972). All of these published Leland's work and *Arena* in particular gave her space. Printing eight poems in the final issue, the brief editorial declared the journal 'proud ... of being friends with good writers like Leland Bardwell, unknown in their country.'

The Autumn 1963 issue of *Arena* had placed John Montague's 'The Siege of Mullingar' on the front page. Its refrain, 'Puritan Ireland's dead and gone/ A myth of O'Connor and O'Faolain' seemed to announce the arrival of the liberated Sixties, even the inevitability of change, 'Everything then/ In our casual morning vision/ Seemed to flow in one direction ...' in Montague's perhaps sceptical words. (Nudging up against Montague's poem on that page is a brief quotation from *Lady Chatterley's Lover*, banned in Britain until 1960, still in 1963 banned in Ireland, though widely read). The frankness, the wild impatience of Leland's poems join up with the spirit of the decade. In one Arena poem she declares 'There is no substitute for sex' ('Lament'), and yet I find a certain distance, almost a coolness in the way she writes about the bohemian life she had been leading. In 'The End of the Party', 'Tom Dick and Harry' claim her:

> 'You'll sleep with me tonight?' they said,
> she, acquiescing, sighed, 'I will
> no other love but yours will suit me quite as well'

But the speaker has her own, different, outlook on the moment,

> 'Then she must choose her bed-mate last,
> to hurt the least the nicest one ...'.

She has '2000 words to write/ before the post goes out tonight', and she declares 'I'm fed up with La Vie de Bohème'. The poem, published in 1965, is dated *London, 1960*, there is a deliberate distancing in space and time. This is not at all a moral distancing, though it crystallises some of the guilt that plagued her (and she remains suspicious of all moralising to the end of her life). It is an assertion of artistic control, and a (partial) refusal of the role of sex object.

It was at this point that I met her and we became friends. Soon we were involved in organizing poetry readings in a Dublin pub, Sinnotts of South King Street, with Pearse Hutchinson and Justin O'Mahony. Her life gradually became more coherent, and her acceptance in a literary scene where new younger writers were moving into view was part of the process. Not that that scene was unruffled; there were certain changes of fashion. The first of the London-based anthologies of Irish poetry, Brendan Kennelly's *Penguin Book of Irish Verse* included only two poems by living women and omitted most of the younger *Arena* poets, though some whose reputations had become unignorable were given space in a later edition. The British publishers were mostly interested in male poets from Northern Ireland, and remained convinced of their superiority. The Dublin publishers regrouped. Dolmen continued to publish; the sober-titled Gallery Press emerged from the more flowery Tara Telephone Publications. The editors of *The Lace Curtain* also ran New Writers' Press, which in 1970 published Bardwell's first book, *The Mad Cyclist*, as well as other collections by the poets of the *Arena* stable around the same time.

Her second collection *The Fly and the Bedbug* (1984) came out from an even smaller and more fragile outfit, Beaver Row Press. Both volumes contain a mixture of the early 1960s poem with subsequent work. This does not mean that she simply remained stuck in the decade of her self-discovery, rather that she went on refining and exploring the insights and the forms of expression that interested her. She ended *A Restless Life* at 1970 because 'I thought it was the end of an era; the Sixties, Bob Dylan, the Beatles, flower power, love' [*Irish Independent,* 14th September 2008, interview with Emily Hourican] but in fact the preoccupations of that era did not evaporate. She firmly references icons of the decade, with a pair of poems in *The Fly and the Bedbug*, 'in memory of Stevie Smith', and a piece, 'Blackbushe' on Bob Dylan's European tour of 1978 ('a million people rise like cattle in an air-raid/ Dylan sings'), which suggests that the hopes of that era had not merely been cast aside:

> She hears as from another star the speakers
> that thunder promises: the dew on the rubbish
> will not always be the dirty dress
> of the pantomime fairy; dates can be lifted
> and set back like starting posts for the sprinters.

The poem is dedicated to her son Nicholas McLachlan, a talented runner; family and poetry are on speaking terms as they had not been earlier.

The appearance of *Dostoevsky's Grave* (1991) suggests a continuing liberation—at least in poetry—from the stresses of her life, though many of the poems come from a fraught enough period. 'Thems your mammy's pills' and 'The Bingo Bus' reflect the shock of her displacement to the newly-built suburbs around Tallaght, after the 1980 eviction, described in an uncollected poem, 'Conversation':

> ... The paper says Mr and Mrs X
> There is no Mr X
> But you and your husband must get out
> I have no husband
> I am the Sheriff
> I have my instructions ...
> You and your husband must leave now
> I already told you
> It says here.....
> I know it says.
> You don't have a husband?
> Yes I mean No.
> So I don't have to leave? ...

From the late 1980s, though, she was able to spend a good deal of time at the Tyrone Guthrie Centre at Annaghmakerrig, Co. Monaghan, which gave her space to write and allowed her to keep her poems in reasonable order. A poem like 'Dawn Guest' marks the discovery of space for contemplation, as it reflects the momentary glimpse of a stag in the garden, 'an episode of tremendous luck'.

The title poem 'Dostoevsky's Grave' comes from her new comparative freedom: to travel alone, to make virtual contact with a literary hero, and to find humour in the misadventure of being locked in a graveyard: 'I rub my fingers/ in his overcoat of stone/ gambling my airline ticket/ and find in the valley/ of my life-line/ the gravel of Baden-Baden.' Being able to connect her own risky life to the obsessive gambling of the great novelist offers a partial validation.

In this context I should underline, if it isn't already evident, that Leland Bardwell can be quite a literary poet. From her rehandling of Greek myth, Orpheus or Leto (and she also wrote a play on Jocasta) to the throwaway last lines conjuring Mary Shelley or Chekhov in poems about a CT scan, or telling of the row that erupts, followed by a conversation with a stranger, when she smokes in a Russian church precinct.

> But socks, he cries, we queue for socks
> Not to mention stockings I say.
> He is shaken with a fine delight
> as we work our way up thighwards
> and I burn slowly—from inside with a scorching love
> from my pocket from the burning cigarette
> and from the sun above my double vented skull.
>
> When we embrace we agree to meet in Yalta
> and feed cyclamen seeds through the eyelids
> of Chekhov's dacha.

The small unexpected gap between her predicament and the bookish allusion stirs the reader alert. More striking still is a poem published in 1989 in *Ambit* but not included in a collection until 2006, in *The Noise of Masonry Settling*. (Like *The White Beach* of 1998, that volume contained many earlier poems.) This one, originally titled 'Hound', is short enough to quote in full:

Insomnia

With me in my truckle bed
there is a hound—
a hound in my head.
There is no gainsaying it—
It howls.

It is the lessons of darkness.

Oh, Couperin,
Couperin le Grand.

When she writes like this, as also in the conversation with the sheriff, and in many more of her later poems, she is bypassing logic. Often to expose the illogicality of society and its gendered assumptions, just as often to bring the reader into a different logic. The allusion here to Couperin's *Leçons de ténèbres* is illogical because the reader may not recognise it, and because it dissociates the 'Readings for Tenebrae' from their liturgical context. It is logical because the dissociation is often what happens when we listen to music—and also when in dreams, or waking from uneasy sleep (the truckle bed suggesting precariousness, discomfort), a phrase we know takes on a different meaning. A poem in *The Mad Cyclist*, 'Precisement' had already referred to the same piece of music, spelling it out literally; she no longer needs to do that. The possibly mysterious statement 'It is the lessons of darkness (singular verb, plural noun) should spur anyone who doesn't know Couperin to go and find him.

These late poems are my favourites, for their agility, their ability to distil experience and to make poetic form work by compression, but I also admire the sheer range and variety of her poems as they are collected here. Together, they are the poems of a life, lived in awareness of all the conflicting systems, of the body, of the mind, society and gender, that leave their mark on the writer and her language.

EDITOR'S NOTE

by

John McLachlan

This book brings together all the poems published by Leland Bardwell, and a large number that were found among her papers after her death. It is a great pleasure to be able to present around 90 poems that were either never seen, or unseen for a half-century, that is, those from periodicals and her papers. In addition, most of her five collections are currently impossible to get hold of, in particular the first two collections, making this an indispensable Bardwell volume.

There is a marked lack of certainty to dating Bardwell's poetry, as she did not date poems or versions of poems except for a small handful of times, and moreover she kept poems for years or decades while considering if they needed a final polish. There is some small degree of detective work possible around typewriters/computers, paper quality, style and subject matter, but it is often horribly rough in its conclusions. The poems have thus been arranged in an approximately chronological order, apart from those pieces from the 1960s which never appeared in collections: most of these have been placed at the end of this book, under the heading 'Other early poems', while some have been kept in their chronological order so as to give a flavour of her writing in that decade.

The poems in her five published collections are presented here intact and in their published order, although *The White Beach* has been broken into decades following the same headings as in the original. That book, published in 1998, brought forth poems never before seen, from the 1960s and later decades, including the long and remarkable 'Kaleidoscope of Childhood In Ireland During the Emergency.' This illustrates the point about her exceptional ability to let poems lie in the drawer for later appraisal and adjustment.

And adjustments are evident over and over when a periodical had a poem that got brought into a later collection. There were often changes: usually small but vital in their effect. Nonetheless, for this edition, we have avoided cluttering the book with all the minor variants, even though they are interesting to those who are very close to the writer. They can perhaps be the basis of some scholarly work later on. A few are included for interest. For example: compare 'Precisement,' published in 1970, with 'Precisely,' published in 2006.

We have not, in this edition, tracked down all the earlier magazine publications of the poems in her five collections, but from the library work that was possible during the preparation of the book, it was clear that the date of a poem is not the same thing as the date of the publication of the collection, and that the variance in this regard can be many years.

In addition, the five collections sometimes dipped into an earlier collection to repeat a poem, and such repetitions have been removed. For example, 'Their Future Hidden To All But Themselves' reappeared in *Dostoevsky's Grave* as 'For Paul and Nessa on the Occasion of their Marriage,' so it is found only on the first appearance in *The Mad Cyclist*, and the index sends the reader to that poem.

Regarding editing and layout, the poems adhere strictly to the published forms in the vast majority of cases, except for spelling corrections and the like. A very few changes have been made to stanza separation where it is suspected from the context that an error had crept in. Regarding initial capitalisation of lines: the dominant style that Leland adopted was to prefer to avoid this, however when she moved to computer use very late in life, they abound. It is assumed that these were unintended and have been removed. A few poems stand out for having capitalised lines to emphasise their relation to song styles, these are retained.

Poems in Periodicals
& from Bardwell's Papers

1960s

Sentimental Journey

To the late starting up of a scooter,
symbol of youth,
they sat on a terrace in Paris,
having driven carelessly,
like people who are in love for the first time.

Although it was a dull foursome,
with the possibility of a cross-flirtation
which came to something
in the Black Forest, while immense pines
claqued at the tips. Utter darkness helps.
The sequence was inevitable,
only one couple clicked.

The two left out meandered dully
round shops, bought useless things,
admired boats, nearly froze to death
on the Brenner Pass. Animal warmth
still an adjunct to sexual heat,
beat in a loft over a cowshed.

All manner of rats and insects crawled
in their folly, they nearly set
the place alight with a candle.

Mixing the wheres with the whys
in every language,
Italy like a cream cake after
the cold puddings of Germany and Austria
befriended them in sunshine.
They drank more coffee than schnapps before
which had speeded up the urgency of desire.

The couples split up in Padua
without rancour or duel
(someone had to have the car)
The winners walked back to Milan
in the holy seclusion of a hot white road,
to catch the Orient Express

Housewives

The angels are staring down at us
with tight sardonic smiles;
they seem inclined to notice,
as pinched behind our curtains
our eyes bleed their salt tears
for the extremes we used to know
before the dust of toil
spread evenly on our minds.

Do they know our dreams
of the whore with the lump on her forehead
who sat for hours at the table
of the café outside the Gare du Nord?
Or of the chalk-faced Americans
who clutched our hands to their thighs,
disparate in their lostness.

In the end we have nothing to show the angels;
the truth has fled on some long-ago night
when we'd left the cold of a cathedral
on a white hot summer's day
in Spain or Greece or Morocco.

We are the photophobes
who sit with our backs to the windows
the too-late wise who kiss the great
with hungry tongues, licking the lies
which we uttered
in a more aesthetic wilderness,
our softness lost

We are the lonely, we cry to the angels;
Penelopes, everlasting, waiting.

The angels are not listening.

The Will, *or* An Old-Fashioned Irish Short Story

The will was read;
ah! bitter chill!
Not a penny?
No, not a farthing!

They'd gambled on its extent,
some fortune, fifty thou?
Well nearly.

Those Victorians were canny,
they still exist in this atomic
year of our Lord.
Thank God, not many.

Oh Lord forgive us for
not behaving conventionally, they said,
we, who followed too much
the devices of our own hearts,
for a start
we did not curry favour. Amen.

A holiday in Greece
Was the least they expected.

Childhood Reminder

I
Amongst the heaps of Engineering Manuals
was Tolstoy's Guerre et Paix 3 Vols:

O! wan guttering clichéd childhood, far away,
my sister and I pissed in the pie-dishes
on my sixth birthday.
In the yard of a Victorian castellated
mansion in Killiney.
It was my idea.

My mother got the dogs out
to try to find us;
we hid for 24 hours
under a box-hedge.

I wanted to make my cousin do it too
but he was too good, or too dull,
or perhaps he already had hairs between his legs
and didn't want us to see.

I loved the taste of my salt tears
afterwards. Not a moment's boredom!

II
Old men are not wise.
Only the very young are wise;
or else old men are too wise to say they are.

III
There is no romance for me
in a graveyard crowded with bones
only in a room crowded with vulgar people
with my lover at the other end.

IV
See-saw Marjorie Daw
Jennie shall have a new master
she shall have a new man a day
and ride on the wings of disaster.

Reward to Finder

The spot I seek is the hour you'll find
I'll seek the hour, you'll find the spot
the spot which was yours will have become mine
and the hour that was mine is now yours
quintessentially the mine and yours mingle
until the hour itself loses its identity
the spot loses its identity
and the will to find the spot is lost
and somewhere between the hour and the spot
is my identity, and your identity
and all your identities

There, to the detriment of ownership
there is no lodgement;
identities laugh in the air
switch on and off like
night fireflies;
arms stretch up like grass in the sun
and in the amalgam of hot air
and listening
opinions, values and processes
of assessing experience
are only as the wheel
being the bark of the tree,
a definition, that in fact
is not a definition
but merely a fault of evolution
elimination, disintegration;
until all our identities are merged
and talking to you
is just like talking to me.

The Circle

In the beginning is the poet
Lonely inviolate; King Cyclops
waving his club at the gate
of his cave. At home to every
sea-runner from outer foam.
His one degenerate eye ready
to pierce the makers
of crudities. Pity
the siren; but that was
another island
                        and besides

then comes hard work
like woman, who puts on virtue
at the drop of a hat; the quick
change artist: or Proteus
Neptune's pal; going down to
the sea in drag.

And then comes sleep that old trier
between crumbs; like one-night-stands
lacerates the flesh and seems
to promote anxiety. Dreams
are the stuff society makes
of necessity; the quick sale
to the first buyer.

Then the next day
when each has had his say in the management
of parts; endless like fiscal dispute
the heart's place is pig-in-the-middle
by the great hole caused by the brain;
all human viscera
have a wall of wonder bone.

And then comes laughter with no excuse
the smudge on the hunt that animals
can't explain; that cuts through life
like a length of hemp; a sign
perhaps, that tension is vertical.

But always the circle,
chasing its crowd-worn tail
that carries the poet,
Lilliputian, unwilling
to understand the necessity
of jumping off.

Trouble In the Flat Above,
or Familiar Irish Short Story

There was an old woman
lived upstairs
she had money from the States
and trouble with her breathing

She was a quare one, the neighbours said
she'd let annyone in, annything in trousers

But no one came
no one came

so she lay in bed and created hell all round . . .

Winter and summer, the fire burned in the grate
at 4 shillings a bag

"Why doesn't she buy it be the ton, the old hag?"
The neighbours said. And the money! The money
she spends on the drop!

Then one day a man came,
O a man.
And he perched on her bed, like a wounded crow.
Nothing like the drop 'ad warm your heart.

But the neighbours said, Tch Tch . . . at her age
disgusting!

And the landlord!
God, he was in a towering rage.
30 bob a week! The flat is worth seven times that
on today's market.
And he stood with his coat collar up
waiting for her to die.

But the man.
The very same man
came every day and perched on her bed.
Go on out of that, she said.

Click click went the neighbours' tongues
like typewriter keys in the hall.

We must get rid of her, they said
into a hospital. Into a home

The grey twinkling eye
Is not for us.
It's dirt in the house.

We have to answer for
the wrath of God

So they all got down on their knees
to pray.

And begob in three days
the wrath of God
came down on cue.

Question

How many hurt-holes-in-the head
Cause psychopathic brain damage
WILL INSULTS KILL

Do you get hurt inside and hard outside
Or hard inside and hurt outside
And which side is the worse to pretend?
And in the knotnow whichside is which.

from

The White Beach

(Salmon Poetry, County Clare, 1998)

*

sixties

Kaleidoscope of Childhood in Ireland During the Emergency

I
And the dead calf's head
was pinned to the foot
of the crib while the pony's ears
peeked over the stable door—
did blood drip down on the white-
washed rough-cast wall
while the pony's frightened eyes
explored the depths of the straw.
Oh, not a girl, the mother angry, cried
as the pelvis stretched again
to expel the afterbirth
Oh not a girl, a boy
might have merited suffering—
pain in the blackened ears like
song in the brain and she slid
her hands through the rumpled
crease of the stomach
flattened now after nine month's hard
like a marrow skin—and then
she knew that she'd get revenge
and call it boy and have it boy
and it would grow male and quick
not female soft that would spare
no-one but itself, and she sought
in her mind for a name that would suit
a boy—hard and generous—
a name of bird or gun
but a changeling, not to expect
affection—you're on your own
the mother, cynical, said
and the baby, cynical, moaned
the final female whinge and
papa banged down the phone.

II
And the mother sedulously kept
the baby away from the breast
and bought a goat that gave
four pints of fine strong milk
a day—the fatted calf had been
a lousy joke of course it
was not born in a stable—oh
no—a damp and blood-stained bed
in some vast hygienic maternity
hall—delivered by rubber gloves
on a midwife's cruel mitts—
you do not scream to disturb
the delights of bearing a child
that you'll grow to hate—
and starve for the sex of pain
like a six inch nail in the head
so the brachycephalic mite
screamed loud and raw and was
out of the shot of ears in a wooden
drawer removed to the top of the house
soon jumped or fell or crawled
from the home-made crib—and they
called it L as it leaned over carved
mahogany stairs that curved to the well
of the house and learned
to embrace the whims of an
adult world—in other words
to lie and kick with an ugly yell
that raised the roof
and then it hid till the guilt
expanded—it had to admit
that it was a boy—not natural—
and would not speak but learned
to read in the Latin tongue.

III
And grandma—the dreadful threat
of shame—leaned over the cot
with the dangerous bars—no good
will come of this—she said

adjusting the iron grey squares
on her head—no pleasant place
ever housed a recalcitrant child
and she whipped her fist across
screaming maw and all the L's
rose up inside O it jumped from
the cot and snatched the text
amor dapis—I'll do it—I'll
have fun if it kills me—it said
and ran and now like fox-cubs
that caper it caught the wind
—the will o' the wisp—that
frightened the wits of the
other kids it sometimes saw
like a dream in the bed—alone I'll
break the valuable delph and
smash the truth from my mother's
ribs and it went to the topmost
branch of the scabrous apple tree
and spat on the distant adult complaints
futura—oh—don't climb up the
tree—it's true you might break
the branch.

IV

At nine it walked in gentleman's clothes
and bore a gentleman's name, Lalande—
eighteenth century astronomer born
at Bourg 'un professeur eminent'—
he busied himself with the comets and
Mercury—Mercury—oh dear god of thieves
he prayed and robbed and lied
O Mercury, messenger of the gods
pay me I shall run I am
Lalande—to watch the stars and
born at Bourg—and I will pluck
the daisies from the grass
while the black dog licks
my cheek—now I am firm and fleet
my feet are narrow my limbs are
slender and strong—I will go

through galaxies and splash through
stars as the beach foam slaps the sand
and the stars will strike the earth
like tomorrow's space locked
and stored as time clocks in.

V

Then indolence—indifference too—
and boredom clouds his mind—he seeks
relief in the cheap thin smoke
pennies snatched from his father's
coat—to hide and lurk in
the winter's grass—brown and curled
as an ancient book, slouched
in a ditch with a passing tramp—
How old are you son?
he answered eleven and offered a pull
on the damp bent fag—he smelled—
the tramp—like a dried sea bed
the boy called him Proteus and combed
the molluscs out of his tangled beard
He snuggled closer into the
sharp scutch-ditch
with the elderly seven-coated man
I love you Proteus—the boy now cried
and his feet could no more run
he'd got so heavy and drab
with the nicotine and the wet
grass drenched his limbs
I'm sunk, he said.

VI

and tiny breasts grew from
his narrow chest that long winter
and bombs fell on another island
The Emergency fell like a brick
all round. Lalande died, the star Mercury
messenger—thief fled into
the skies and the boy hid his breasts
and between his legs he put rags
which turned orange—red—then

black—and stank—and he threw
them over the hen-coop wire
dug half a hole in the muck,
in the yellow-smelling hen-shit—
It's happened, the mother said—No!
No! I deny, he answered—I cut my leg
on the netting wire and bowing like
an apostrophe he turned and ran again.

VII

And now boy/girl it did not trust
it learnt new words like scavenge—poison
it put berries in its matted hair
it tied up the riverreeds and lay
under the snowberries to burst
between finger and thumb and spurt
cream—it is cow-poison, see
it squelches like the udder
of the mad white cow that crosses
the moon—and money became as important
as the Latin homework and the lame
old dog—mongrel—that was christened
Bran.

VIII

Then at thirteen her name is
Lalage—she puts on long skinny
dresses with stripes—she wears
silk stockings and paints her
face in the bus from school—
she tenders half fare and smokes
behind filthy exercise books of don'ts
Do not cross the road
when you see the clergyman coming
Do not subsume your guilt
your hormones will split on you
Do not announce your equations
to the vigil-keeper—stone breakers
guides—ribbon men—you meet by

the way side. Do not do not—do not
open the book at the bus-stop it has
you by rote—it reads—there are
more than eight furlongs in the
eye long waste of seeing—two
perches
in the dried up shibboleth
of the adult mind—twenty-
hundred days in the tonal
monotony of adolescence avoir du
pois—weight—wait there is more
heavy stuff—nits in the hair that smells
of paraffin—black smears like hammer—
blows in the convex shelter
of the neck—legions of blackheads
down the delicate abrasion of the nose—
Oh noise—O—of thinking she's a girl
what must the boys—oh no—think of
her—luckily she knows none—a socio-
logical stratum about which a mist
of ignorance steams—you can keep them—
a speculation—like what the parents—
now almost human—I mean—with all
that chatter about politics—mean
I mean—do—do they ever—Oh no
the very thought of it!

IX
Meanwhile the microscopic
nerve-cells—called neurons—of
which there are billions
systematically linked together—Nature
takes care—she murmured—chewing on
a Mars Bar—the wrapper caught—
hovered twirled fled on the wind—the
bus swerved—You may only enter
Paradise if—only enter Paradise if
you've been there before—when
she eloped from the bus she cried
Come all ye Yanks—war-dodgers—snivelling

mittel-European refugees—English
prisoners of war—Germans—On parole
from the sheep-short grass
of the Curragh—try me
I'm Locusta—known for my poisons
help-meet of Nero—and Laodice
 sometimes called
Electra—will with my brother—
two-bit moralist—not under
any circs—try me I can ride—
swim—run—am fleet as a boy—was
a boy—I can play the piano and dodge
the fine rain that falls lightly
on my Latin mistress—Amo—
Miss White—Amo—Miss White Pulchra
est—Irish boys are hell—
but only the wind flapped answer and
the hemiptera made sucking sound
on the tight white skin of her skull.

X

Now she curled in the circum-
volution of the dog-eared books—
there was catharsis if you like
—not the night bell clang of the church
clock reminding you'll not make the
early bus—fat tallow on the pillow-
case under Poe—Tales of Imagination—
or—worse still—the game is
—the game is—up—not worth
the candle—Kafka F., Dostoevsky F.
have snuffed it Rosa Luxemburg and those
hard working Italians who fought for
the poor were stuffed or topped or
burnt by electricity—Millions
of volts according to State—Ho America
our new big movie-scene Mitch for Garbo
Claudette America of the automobile
apartments—ice-boxes—elevators
foxy little husbands eaten by
big fat Blue Haired Mommas

T. Williams—E. O'Neill
TELL ALL—come to Leixlip
we'll sell you anything from
a bull dozer to a bull terrier dear—
O dear—dear America you are over-
doing it—you've more cars
eat more bright red beef
than anywhere else put together
and two billion dollars spent on cos-
metics—lips—cheeks—eyelashes
as unlikely as a mid-wife's sex-
fantasies—powder paint lip-
stick—brushed on delicately not
jammed on like we do it—two Donald
Ducks kissing on the cartoons
perms—straighteners—grease—eye-
shadow—and all those lovely shan-
gri la creams/Tír na nÓg here
I came watch those lines wrinkles
psoriasis spots—tumours cancers
lifted like magic plain envelope results guaranteed we'll
comb out your
body odour—note the spelling—
we will exterminate breasts—
babies—or any other
minor growth or irritation
Phew Satan—consider me an applicant
for a new lease of life.

XI
And so Satan—so cunning said
You've asked for it I'm punning
on the highway with the great Cave
boy—Clergyman's son—myopic
barely—but clean with pointed ears
like bat's wings—there's things
you should know about, baby—he's
not Gary Cooper or even James Mason
much less Raskolnikov—but he'll give it
to you hot and proper in his Trinity
rooms—zooms—Lalage—Laodice—dark-

robed Leto—Lucretia—the lot arrived
panting—not to be kept waiting another
second in stained-brown gym-tunic late
for school ready to overlook all poss-
ible flaws in the execution of her De-
flowering—capital letter—better
never than late—what a let-down
and no bed just the tea stained
draining board or else the floor—cold—
you've said it—I've changed my mind
my grandfather is dead—Today
is the Ides of April the month of Venus—*Quam*
Pulchrissima Virginem he said crunching
her narrow bones and scattering them
on the hard floor Tomorrow—she
cried—I'd die sooner—Domani
e troppo tarde—he said—You've
a nerve—she said simulating courage
of a last minute variety—Piety
was never your strong point—he
said—reverting to English—I'm off
she said. She went—Back to Satan
said—There's some mistake—I
don't seem to go for it after all
I guessed you'd be like that Satan
replied his face creaming over
with a wily smile—how much your soul's
quarter then for old Beelzebub—eh?
Annihilated yet curious she murmured I
Locusta ought to have a career
Love-squeaked Satan—ten decibels
later she said—What about
shorthand-typing? Love squeaked
the fork-tailed menace—no no—anything
else—a trip to Venice after
the war—meanwhile my Inter-inter
alia—Ha ha—you'll never pass
your Irish is terrible.

XII

But unfortunately that thick
word truth will out she'd
as usual lied did not—in fact—
say what she thought she had—let alone
pretended to herself—the devil and
all his works—that she's said
she had not said any of the above
things to the original cave-boy Trinity
raper in chief for fair play Tarquinius
Lucretia vim—ha—attulit
on the highway she in fact had lacked
the courage to refuse and now nightly
prayed—Lord—don't let it happen
There are always the Cliffs of Moher
no-one ever jumped backwards
up those grey-flensed Ireland's
answer to the New York State Building
another eighteen days before I'll
know for certain—and Jesus—
what about Grandma?

XIII

The sunshine strikes ricochets on
the gay gun-metal pavement in College
Green—eyes right—like a Scout—
girl—Lalage—ragazza—better
Laodice—but fears Orestes now older
student—falconer—lurking over
the sister's guilt—O Agamemnon O
Clytemnestra she shouts to the
dead blue sky while scurrilous clouds
play hill and cheek with the sunstriped
warning—all normal people scurrying
late—but pure—no crippling dread—
she—to everyone of them a load—
an eyesore—embarrassment—Grafton Street
Mitchell's—thin feet scudding hard—
O Woolworth's land of ear-rings and
brooches—bangles heavy with charms—
one for every birth day—one—

for her a fish—pellucid sea—
Nereis—daughter of Neptune receive me
your wet arms will stroke me like strings
of emerald beads—wind them about
my body till the dead weed drags me
down in the depth of your rock
swollen like water forced from
the earth by the satellite Icarus
until a false god will cry Noah
save the clean ones—but Laodice
cries to be her own her brother to
become again a boy and when the moon
is round and she is free—she
will once more squander her limbs to
the crazy air—tinker—daughter of sand
son to the sunflower—tropist and
she will turn to the burning orb—
barb—needle or hazel-stick twin to
herself entwined in the freedom of
trading form with mind—tendering
each delicate hair—thin foliole ray—
to breathe—to go faster than sound
than light—than gravity—
then no lecherous grave will shout
her names—Locusta will live
Laodice—Leto—of the night
Even Lucretia—but mostly will
the astronomer Lalande—of Bourg
arise to bless his birth O
how pale and full and sure
is the moon that slides in
the purple night—night star
of morning Venus—his aide—
guide of mariners—hour long vigil
of fear to devouring hope—life IS
when death breaks foul in the mouth
like an old man's failing gasp. Turn
like time from the tortured lips
of the wrinkled hag.

XIV

But soon she is sunflower—tropist—
and turns again—back to the wind—
dark sea—subsumation of still wind
weed and fissure—a gin—adread
of scorn—pleasure of need—O
she will want and want—desire is the
drought that blames the desert—reflecting
men who build of sand and thunder
the burial banns to the gaunt and silent mob.

XV

And then there was freedom of a kind
dark circle of dread evicted from
the mind—the moon had fled
Laodice sought herself—her real
brother Orestes—they will revenge
the father's death in a child-worn
mind—soon or never—but
will one day join—now she waits
on the drydock's edge
the sledge hammer beats like a gong
in her head—one day they will
sing me Electra—but now I
am boy again—brother sister—all—
I am—Orestes—he sings as he tried
the bridle paths and lies in the
shade of elm and beech—never
again will they catch him out
he bows to magpie and calls to
thrush—bluebird carrion or winter crow
learns to whistle and tread like
a boy—hands in pockets—lurch and
kick—What an atrocious piece of luck he
says—subsides in a ditch with a book.

Message for Dickie

'Goodbye little yellow bird'
—Victorian Music Hall song

Here is a sort of conspiracy
a poem that will steal around you
like your lover's arms.
A poem, without literary sentences,
that might only hover and pick at the truth
like moths around Marlene Dietrich.

I love you, Richard
like I love old steam trains
and the memory of beer bottle tops
sticking to the carpet
in Lower Leeson Street.
You know that freedom
is something for the birds
and if once in a while
you open the cage of the canary
they'll throw the square root
of bureaucracy at you
and they'll strap you
on to the metal horses
and absent minded stereo sounds
will make the fifth ending.

To Robert MacBryde, Died May 1966

As each one is guided by his own mad star
so, Robert, too soon hurled into the night.
Your feet, leaf-light, side-stepped too late.

Chaining history to your Achilles Shield,
fashioned by your one-god, Hephaistos,
who yet extracted for his grasses your wild flowers.
Like gazing from a Míro to a mirror.

Thus did you have to wander always
and alone were by wonder driven.

Dance Robert, nowhere now,

all is forgiven.

Returning Home

She returned to the house, the house, the house
where she was born, grew into her brothers' clothes
and fought the enemies.
Where the iron bed
was a Sultan's gate
where Gaugin's Polynesian wife
hung from the scabrous apple tree
and the last bus missed and the hinges shrieked
and the flags were cracked and the stairway creaked.

She'd return to the house
with the answering ass and the putrid tank
the slimey strawberry-coloured sides
where she'd slithered in in her brother's clothes
and was afraid to go in with the dreadful stink
that rose from her garments
covered in autumn leaves

She'd see the old place again
to get the necessary pang
that would subsidise her normal pain.
Fine, she thought, fine,
the place will have fallen, anyway.

She approached the town planning.
The new road pressed in, a tidal wave,
factories fanning aggressively;
boxes of precision, a hemisphere
of no-man's land.
Teenagers rushed out with love in their buckets
to pour on her shadow and the houses
bowed to her sightless and closed.

At last the house,
the granite stones had been scrubbed
pointed—O Moon, O Jaguar
22 litres, 80 degrees from the door
O apple green Georgian asphalt drive
crush her feet! She pressed the bell.
Who shall I say—a voice from hell.
Who indeed, she said. We don't drown, it said
only burn, but step inside.

Her host sat naked under a sun ray lamp.
Yes? he said with a masterful smile.
It's just my lies, she said, I left behind
I can't have them lying around all over the place
He laughed at her pun, Pernod?
he suggested hostfully
his body dappled with healthy tan,
I'm a man, he said, thumping his breast.
I'll make you an offer for the best lie,
she said. Your happy past?
he asked. By now he was dressed
a business man to his socks—
his lips the cream of a wily smile.
How much? A barrel of winter charm
a dead rat and a rusty nail.
Done, he said, and took her arm.

Locked in his Jaguar power dream
She would go his way
to the speculator's dead man's hole
where he prized his life
to its iron grey soul.
She laid her head on his £100 shoulder.
Never. He drew to a stop.
The plan of the engine is God.

Leixlip and the Rye

Leixlip, my first and great and only love,
I wish I could describe the street
just house by house.
Or first the largest squarest Georgian
which they messed with pipes outside;
a wasted garden back and front.

Or begin with the bridge
before the hydro-electric scheme
shut off the water, dirtied its bed
and left a tray of weeds.

From the bridge, the castle
gay in places, different faces
of granite dragged by local labour;
a tiny harbour for the castle boat.

But no-one wrote about the Rye;

The Liffey, in every loving curve
is praised so much (leave out
the Salmon Leap, which now
is quite a pleasant engineering feat
while salmon must go underneath
to spawn.)

Wondering wandering tributary
whose source lies somewhere near Kilcock.
Through your valleys and Moyvalley
watering Carton's gardens,
all the Dukes of Leinster washed;
an Empress jumped you once.

You crushed out the gravel
under the royal canal
driving a bargain into the fields of Confey.
And there at the castle gates of Leixlip
roared your allegiance with the Liffey
with the little bridge at the castle gates,

a pub on either side,
where a lady ran guns in the troubles
and other ladies cried,
watching their Georgian mansions crumble;
a humble stream that cut their Anglo-Irish meadows
with reeds and dragonflies and otters,
who played briefly in their reason.
And the ladies waited patiently
for the start of the hunting season.

from

The Mad Cyclist

(New Writers' Press, Dublin 1970)

Kafka Revisited

The old child
lay dying of insomnia
too tired to get up
and put out the light
found the interpretation
of experience, which
is called intelligence,
too boring
to live for;
would choose to climb back
into dream; but
dreams like drains
take ordure;
“small doings”,
and the world is busy;
strangers, probably relatives
would likely interfere.

So the child grew
to age in dilemma
remaining the same
but wishing to change
out of all recognition;
discarded suicide
as out of date
and the cause for strangers’
inconceivable rancour.

Innocents

In B movies
they use tomato ketchup.
In art films
they use an expensive
cosmetic
paint,
not even
obtainable
in Ireland.

In real life
they use
blood.

Coole, September 1968

It was at Coole,
how could I cool, say
to-day
is of yesterday.

Five swans, two parent birds,
strike out from the shore
Augusta's apples,
those glorious pippins,
are sour,

A blind man swills
his poitín barrels
"Eight hundred pounds
to the Forestry;
it would have fallen anyway."

The blackberries grow lush
in the drawing room
thorn everywhere,
"Where is the exquisite pale shell?"
It is three cracked tiles
and a broken wall.

The swans call;
they are not muted
specially imported, you said
by Henry the Second.

Coole Tree, the arrow says
I search for Lady Gregory's
greengages
while the smell of box
"makes a labyrinth of the mind."
What is a poet
"who lives on grubs and flies
And feeds the heart on fantasies?"

The blind man chucks his horse
"come build in the empty house"
without patrons, poets!
Hard by in Ennis, they
are doing their nuts
two Merry men have
fisticuffs about another.

WBY on the tree
we could not find the plums
the Forestry have dug them up
but the beech can only live
200 years in Ireland.
It can't withstand the damp
the tree is dying.

"A passing word"
from the blind man
did you ever taste it,
the Mountain Dew?

We are tourists;
is the "age" or the poet dead ?

For the Shade of F. Scott Fitzgerald

Etiolated I get up each morning
from my basement in Low Leeson Street,
sometimes it is afternoon when I surface.

Where things are normal for a few
at street-level, the sun perhaps may shine
but warmth can be bought
by cheque-book or tongue.

I stand aside in shops
making my fiscal offerings
for necessities,
remembering the givers and the takers
are always with us
with their patterns and their graphs.

It is safer to laugh at the patient
whose lovers may get angry
if their breakfast is also late.

The Mad Cyclist

The wind blew West from the sun
on the force of the oncoming pedaller
at 400 revs per m;
Exceeding the navicular limit
she steered through the middle
of buses and hot summer skins
of the addle of stammering sex
and the men with wallets
that split at the seams
and are worn like life preservers.

This fantoccini on wheels
was clean as their short plump limbs
harboured sweat in the toes of their socks;
she was fast as the slow dawning leers
disguised their political cramps;
and funny, flashing past like the Enterprise
bringing the business men in
in a merciless Mondaying manner
as they behind blocked in a row
who, thanks to their waterless tanks
were shrunken and human piranha

Such arrogance must be prevented
such unnatural practices stopped
or have her certificated
for putative felo-de-se
but she with her revs circumvented
their aims and cried "ou est mon velo?"
like Cocteau to Diaghilev
when the latter said 'J'suis étonné.

And she sped past
left them astonished
with the swoon of her pupils
balancing her country pride
on a mirage de convenance.

Then we'll have her obfuscated
in the quicksands of modern suburbia
they conceived a magnificent plot
of creating a labyrinth
in an anonymous building estate
and providing a motorized minotaur
which sooner or later should eat her.

But she threaded her way
through the eye
with miraculous wisdom
descending the hill
the latest escarpment
of souls in cement
(her movements inclining to skill)

Yet in spite of her feral intensity
she chose to despair
on a wintry night in July
the moment that Aldrin and Armstrong
stepped off the moon.
she steered her base-metal bicycle
out of the sterile orb
and bumped in the rut she was in
to the last still lake that made light
leaving the tarry academized snake
propounding a theory
that everything might have been bought with a bike
if time had allowed her to think.
With the final escalibrous flash
of the handlebars
the jewels of poverty sank.

Abortion

An equivocal situation:
no coffin, casket, or pertinent
corner in a mortuary.
The saliva of love
from between his lips
like her hot wet thighs
made a little death.
From Earth to Earth
now she lies
with gathering hips
in her labour of blood
like April perpetually
waiting; and sentient
of the next insemination.

Cinema 70

In the movies the goodies got the witch
they belted her with their moral superiority
so she got the hell out;
the sound men and the sparks had had a ball
and the director stopped tearing up paper
while he thanked everyone.
They folded their gear and took it
beyond the essence of believing.

In the dust and dark of the studio
the ghosts of the copulating couples
settled down to acknowledge
the past as valid; although
freedom was a better lie.

The director went out into winter
so tired he could barely move
the trees leaned on him like sick vultures
he was fed-up making B movies.

The following day he rose at 5;
he tore up six unit call-sheets
and the menu for yesterday's lunch;
he got on the blower to his backer
and upped his expenses £20.

He was on the set at the dot of six
(the unit and the cast had fierce hangovers)
especially the female lead.
The director was relentless:

Learn your lesson on the marriage bed, mistress,
lie well and hide your mercy under the mattress.
(page one of the script; the basic four-letter
suffering invented by tubercular Egyptian princes
5000 years B.C.)

So, because you understand
you have invented a game:
blind-man's-buff in the hall of mirrors

if the bandage slips they'll see your eyes,
frightened, accusing or acquiescent,
but never understanding
they don't know you understand
there's no reflection on the mirror.

If love has been killed by love
it is hidden like crystal into water
take it smooth from the river
and warm the crystal in your palm;
name it
You will give out puffs of perfume
like the daughters of the rich
then summer will kill the flowers
and the black grass pencils, the horizon.
You will put your blood on the rod
and say "carry away the birth,
the birth is yours."
and dry your hands in the fire
if the blood has stained the sheets.

Proteus changed his costume
for the nth time, saying
"some people are never satisfied."
The female lead screamed "it's a lie,
a stupid lie. Who do you think you are?
Fellini? Bergman?"
The day wore on as planned;
the crowd extras yawned
into overtime.

The director embraced his chihuahua;
now that he was going to be famous
he had nothing to live for;
he had torn up the flooring
of his Mercedes 230 S.E.
and the extended budget by mistake.

He went into the empty studio
and squelched round on the flat sausage rolls
he overheard a conversation being conducted
by one of the copulating couples,
heretofore mentioned;

"Now that the movie is re-wound
what'll you do
Prisoner of the Snow Queen?
Will you melt at your brother's kiss?"

"No, that'd be too warm."

"Will you wash the dead horse
and stretch the skins in the sun,
rider?"
"No, that'd be too healthy."

"Will you cut the shroud on the cross
so that it hangs well,
seamstress?"

"No, it might look like a loin cloth."

The director cast round for some paper
but the sparks had thrown the main switch
(it wasn't his job to know what that was)
he made a mental note to change his psychiatrist;
this therapy was tedious.
He asked the copulating couples to shut up a minute
so as he could get his bearings;
as then he threaded his way through the broken paper cups
and the leads from the dead brutes;
he ripped up his clothing;
feeling no better, he died.

There was a tremendous funeral;
the company was drunk for a week
The female lead went to bed with the wardrobe master
by mistake; she thought he was Proteus;
the newsmen never had it so good.

Months later some joker wrote on his tombstone
"Understanding blew his mind."

Passing the Time

for Bob Dylan

Here's the train, said Desolation
Death said, Pointless information.
I said, That's sentiment
of premature departure;
the truth is difficult.
But Desolation was too indolent
to listen to the future

Rejection

for Geoffrey Firmin

1. The worm comes
not Blakean
invisible
there

The childbird feasts
accepts from the parent
until

Full of worms
it puts on feathers
says

To fly
I have eaten
the visible

The invisible
is the parent's
funeral

2. Had the world coped
shared his battle
for the survival
of the human consciousness
had he not bored
his listeners to tears
weighing them down
with the dram
of his sufferings
had they recognized
his resources for escape
from bat, flea or church
as a frail return
into agenbite
had they realised
between drink and drink
the exquisite harmony
of his reason's capabilities
Had the contumacious barflies
interpreted
his conundrum differently
it could have been they
not he, who offered
rejection.

In the Sepulchre There Was Time

In the sepulchre there was time
and in the rock there was water
and that was long ago.

When underneath logos
a kind of living worked;
worked, yes, like the ants
hard at it, always hard at it

The cities were jewels
full of Florentine wonder
and the paths were snakes
purposefully hissing outwards.

A tintinnabulation in a tiny harbour
was like the surprise of no foreknowledge
and the power of remaining;
the fronds, the sinuous sweeping waves
disturbed without distorting.

And that was long ago.

They were happy then on their cloud
there were books a-plenty
Oh, they're not blaming the books.
But the sun curled up the paper

So they made a fork: a tight
cirrus trident held aloft
and sank like Neptune into an aqueous nature
womb-like; for there was no returning.

But they shall return, basefully
intent, over-bred, and burdened;
the skinny claws of their ancestors
will dig holes in their flesh;
The had and have-not breeding
inwards, like a fire that burns the earth
and therefore does not burn,
For they don't believe in Hell
and that makes me laugh.

And they will laugh
Like donkeys laugh when they bray
(they say it augurs rain).

only bugs fall like rain
on a bed in Holloway
if only the state
would see to the ceiling.
The annual ceiling-fall
gets greater every year!
And that's not funny either.

The strains of a distance
got, ho, so romantic
strings plucked or lightly
passed over, fingers straying
like an idle tracing in the sand
betraying a sun that pierced the skin.

So they made a doxology of the past
like an old whore gone to religion,
table turning or advanced astrology.

Then the calf of reason
was fatted up again
They cut off the limbs and the hands.
especially the hands;
they gave their money to the butchers
who snatched the fiscal offerings
and threw the bones in the sawdust.
The warm round mouths closed
like wounds, ill stitched by jungle surgeons
who wear no masks.

The lonely amputator whispers

It was long ago in the sepulchre
when there was water in the rock.

Dilemma

Presuming to change me was
what you wanted;
having changed me
and me unwilling
to be changed.
And you not recognizing
that you had changed me
what you changed me into was
not what you wanted.

Goethe Said: Beware of What You Want When You're an Adolescent: You'll Get It in Middle Age

Friend Goethe:
Time is the only evil
for it evicts its wonderings,
God's leavings on the frightened trees:
Youth's precepts' septimal wanderings.
Zero speaks with a tongue of gold:
the old and getting old
will clutch precision's circus hand
with selfish iridescent fingers
Laughter grinds out its faithful dirge
money's obscene autolatry.
But the talking, Jesus
the talking can never stop:
an amalgam, an innocence, a grief
of so-called enemies
and so-called friends.

Better the brands of memory
make suns in a dying fire.

Their Future Hidden to All But Themselves

Apart, they tore the ropes asunder
and clearing the decks, each
cast a net in his own turbulent mind;
there, revealed a high solitude
as equivocal as a war to end wars
Cast again for certainty, and found
memories, old as an ill-tuned drawing room piano;
cast again for beauty, and found
the petals of asters:
each petal as thin
as a strand of the future.

They shall weave with the petals of asters
the skin of a shirt.

Also appeared in *Dostoevsky's Grave* as "For Paul and Nessa"

For Ruth Ellis

In Camden Street, London, N.7
and that was long before
marching became the norm
a brisk watery sun
rose, surly, on a bank of trees.

As hysteria mounted,
took over the precinct
like a burning house
in the mess of dogs
and bulging rubber faces.
The schoolkids mitched
bursting into the clamour
with their clear morning faces
like soap-bubbles in the sun.
crying 'REPRIEVE'
and half of them did not know
the meaning of the word.

In the breakfast of their equal loss
The Queen
The Home Secretary
and Ruth Ellis
had eaten well

That was the latest news

Sensational

Please Mr. Pierrepoint
another lover died outside a Hampstead pub
who took the trade of dalliance and sport;
but eternity plays in a jealous mart
we kill for stupidity, not for love.

From hopelessness to helplessness,
from dearth to dearth returned.

But behind the useless bulging of that oaken door
somewhere, undefeated, the hangman stands,
immutable as a snowman.

If her rope is a makeshift cross
what good comes out of a tragedy that's pure
or a comedy that's harsh?

Precisement

Of course
        all things are rich to me,
        precision equally is correct;
        the muscles of a boy's back
        in early Latin sun
        the line of a Bentley tourer,
        resting blandly in a Georgian square;
        not to mention the neck
        of a racehorse,
        money itself,
        the ablative absolute,
        white in the sun,
        the cold of a cathedral,
        the smell of a new tennis ball &
        Couperin's Leçons de ténèbres.

But if I were rich
I should buy:

        a new solicitor
        a good excuse,
        a soft path to walk upon
        & 25 pairs of shoes.

Still I have seen
the boy, the Bentley and the racehorse;
I have felt money and the cold
of a cathedral,
I have smelled the tennis ball
and heard Couperin's
Leçons des ténèbres.

I hope that I may never grow
too old to go barefoot.

They Put a Bed in the Passage

On First Looking into St. Pat's

They put a bed in the passage
and said "lie down"
Until a purple vacuum created its fulcrum:
Glory, glory, glory
to the spring, not this side
of Thomas Street;
for we don't believe in flowers;

they gave us the dark side of the moon
to live upon
and not content with that
they quartered it till
it was like a bad banana.
There we clung together
as far apart as possible
till the others came;
they brought ichor in their syringes
these dark venal furtive earth-men
and we admired them
like we admire Messrs. Stafford, Young and Cernan
but we don't envy them.

For they shall return whence they came
like landlords who get no rent.
But we promised we'd pay the rent
and we believed it. But we didn't do it.

So that's why they kept coming back.

Flowers for Three Dead Men

I
was a low-sized lad from Belfast
who made me along the quays
on a night and a day against
arm or winch or spar
or something cold like a midnight steel
where a seagull dips
and waters discreetly lap
as the Liffey's lazy mouth
yawns into a sea.
We kipped in a B. & B.
the following night
between sheets where emigrants'
flea-blood spots were
each like a tache or mote;
there we mingled for twelve hours full
till a lady in lavender dress
announced time was up.
A dread to a girl; besides
he was drunk when he left.

II
the best, was a Norfolk man—a host
to his loves, all surl and sex
like a black-skinned man on a furl.
A giant 6 ft. 3 in his sox.
He spoke not of love for speaking destroys
(he was intelligent as well!)
yet we sailed by a moon on a cirrus dream
with Icarus wings for seven years
till the sun.

III
had it away with my friends,
delightful in a daisy-way
but this limited our relationship
and debt did us part.

Tiny lifeless anemone hurts.

Poems in Periodicals
& from Bardwell's Papers

Early 1970s

The Dead

My muse invites me to forget my debts,
pile up more enemies.

Invoke the few

who are helpful, generous
but not always honest.
To make secrets for the few
like "whispering time".

But the few are filtered
and numbered in the funerals.
They follow the coffins.

So I pacify my muse
by joining the cortège
and sprinkling my secrets to the mourners
like the violets of the poor.

In this way then I too
may take my balance from the dead,
measurable only as with the drachma
of the silversmith,
that they in immobility
lie fortunate;

Only the dead are sane.

They'd Been At It for Weeks

The sun poured in at an angle
on the pile of unwashed plates
in the sink, the film of grease
carried an odd carrot. The New States-
man lay between them. The triangle
him, her and her, and increas-
ingly frequent discussion. Right
and wrong, as if they were real
truths, not ethics, a slight
variant on the traumatic ordeal
each of them suffered separately
the slant it cast on their own
actions that each thought the other
merely capable of; at the end of her tether
she shouted: go and fuck her then;
the sun went out with a bang
and the rain started pissing
down the window like hysterical laughter
dirty and wet the children came
into the room; the tame
monkey hopped up the hole in the drain
and landed in the new stuffed kang-
aroo she had bought the baby, the softer
toys, recommended in last week's coloured sup.
You stupid bitch, I don't give a tup-
penny God's curse on your opinions, if
you had a tittle of wit you'd know when
to shut up. He got up and rather stiff-
ly, made a dignified exit. Men,
how are you, she told the monkey,
the tears galloping down her cheeks.

Pisces

Piscean the body
light as paper
swam through
the pawn-broker's eye
and fell in a blob
of inked-in street

Piscean the heart
shut fast on
the scrivener's tray
like a bivalve on
the ocean's feet

And Piscean the mind
as it floats, sly
nothing paid for
or laid in a winding sheet.

The Novelist

"Take off your prose,"
the poet said to the prose-writer
"The formula proves," said the latter
in worsted paperback book
form. "No harm," said the poet
resuming his pint; but
the insult uneasily met
"Get you," he said,
"Bum, layabout, lush."

There was a general hush.
The barman stiffened in his tracks;
"Mind your backs," he said
brushing past peacemakers
and piss artists.

The novelist rose
and adjusted his prosings
"MY books are my bread."
"Should be the other way round."
the poet, chortling, said.

The novelist padded his way
through the luminous Dublin
late night opening mouth
to alleviate his mortal
drouth, he went
into the golden palaces.

Heaven-sent cheque-book man,
what a tread! How sure
of himself. Here
where the sun is a neon sigh
he set himself up.
A gay spender; and eccentric,
high on a hundred-guinea suit.

Motor Accident

The metal dancers
have folded their bodies
the music is over.
They have kissed
and made pictures
on the road as rich
as sandstone and
maps of poppy-red
and lime-green.

Long ago the mothers
folded their bodies
when the music was over.
They have not kissed
anyone since their children
grew, but continue
the pantomime of
their own silent deaths.

The Poet Contemplates Suicide

The children look away embarrassed
The boom of my pulse has woken them up
valium might have been prescribed
if the doctor had remained
but the pain was an embarrassment to him
and he made it plain
that such a noise caused by a beating pulse
was a public nuisance
and likely to be a strain
on the neighbours
he could of course take
extreme measures and remove
by surgery, the brain.

O yes I cried hastily I'm a menace
above or below or just passing through
if a sharp knife could be of assistance
you won't see the tears on my face—
with a quick incision of the viscera could be removed
and any chemical reaction
would be due to my decision
it would not leave a stain
on the medical profession
or even cause derision

But the doctor said
"Don't always turn things to your advantage
suicide isn't the only syndrome
of poetry's squalid reaction
They bottled Byron's brain
and put Shelley's head in a hatbox
and Keats threw his dinner
out of the window to annoy the cook
when he was on the brink of death himself
and none of these men by hook or crook
could be said to have committed good
old felo de se." The doctor subsided.
I took the joke and cut it in half
inside the joke was another
and another and yet another and
there are still plenty of good jokes left
in the poetic pression.

The Dream

Give me the plankton
        and lead me to another ocean
"said the whale". Mammal—brother
        ton upon ton of
it is makebelieve
        too large to live

A fan like a Japanese gentleman
        might donate freely—that is
a ray's ribs—comb on comb
        a fan or an excuse—four black pawns
to the enemy—please don't take
        them till you have won the arms race

But there is too much mud in the tunnel
        it glues down the feet
the enemy is away in front
        let me follow O let me follow

The Awakening

I comb the pawns from the pillow
        the angle of light—pre-dawn
is regular—fawn—the air is swollen
        I remember a pharoah who rose early
one morning—hot day—much work to be done
        yet, on the one beyond Cheops
and asks his slave—a boy less than seven
        to bring the litter

I do not like this story

From Leitrim to Baggot Street Hospital

We have tried the past and it failed
and brought the morning into the hand
—the dark May bush is stripped
down to its winter thorn—

"Much wine was drunk the previous night"
the empty room is scarred and stales
—the list of rules has been analysed
the consultant describes another notch
(he has pressed his successful suit)
the orderly orderly bows
and the final lift whines up

Dionysos is dead
before age has swallowed sense

"there are no scarecrows left
in the Leitrim fields"

The simple fraction of failure
has subtracted the jester's cup
has isolated each bell
like the friend of the moon:
the country child that delights
In a sky-smooth empty road

"there are no scarecrows left
in the Leitrim fields"

Even the lover's hand has grasped remorse

When granite lies in the gut
—the brazen thump of the heart
is aligned to the surgeon's smile—

the five of spades turns up as the picture falls

"There are no scarecrows left
in the Leitrim fields."

Mountain Funeral

for John Stewart Collis

Protestants mourn in abstracted fashion
they do not argue about the will
nor gossip freely about new wives
old ways—they say that blood
is thicker than water and the 'one for sorrow'
bird came to Ireland with Cromwell
and brought the hard god with him—
who are they to twist history
or favour the quick-trading Dane—
the indolent Celt—they cannot absorb
shock for it leaves them frozen
and sentimental about animals or the snipe
that flashes past like a message—
time's passage?

The volcanic waste whose last rumble
was heard in a distant millennium
has much time on hand to absorb
the shocked and muted group whose
blood lies in the light oak box—
even the sheep have been tidied up
to allow for cars whose metal
shock absorbers bounce at risk
on mountain mud and rut and rock
of ages—ages cleft?

Protected by abstractions—full
of emotion that makes adrenaline flow
the shared blood is blood real and love
steals round like an egocentric child
who'll do anything for attention
—innocent of old feuds—unfair
proportions—fame or fiscal stability—
no change—no change whatsoever
from one generation to the next.
They are struck by this new sharp truth
that stands out like grey hair on a young face.
Who is forlorn, lies later—
forlorn, lies

Amanda Sheridan

"There she goes,
in the flower of her sixties
and multi-channel as well.
Not a ha'porth wrong with her.
They say she has a fortune put away."

Amanda Sheridan emerged from
the dustbowl of her living room
in Leeson Street—ribbon of stability
take the baskets of loneliness
with her and follow her to the supermarket
Amanda Sheridan buys fish fingers
(the small packet) and one tin of dog-food
(the sister went last year) she has orange
lipstick and a voice like a tennis tournament
thirty years in the civil service (now retired)
Amanda Sheridan doesn't give a damn.

Do you think the lousy eight pounds
she cashes each week make a ha'porth of difference?
Amanda Sheridan loves her dog.
Amanda Sheridan's dog, like a Russian
stalks her heels enormously. Smells
and studies in Leeson Street.
He puts up with it.
He lifts his leg on a passing Jesuit
Amanda Sheridan booms: "Dear dear,
Sorry Father!" The priest, ridden
with study, hurries by.

Yesterday they found her, Amanda Sheridan
a lump on the floor. The overstuffed
rubbish bins breathe: Amanda!

from

The White Beach

(Salmon Poetry, 1998)

*

seventies

And Hyde House Comes Tumbling Down

Business is business
(Death and destruction).

I watched from my yard
(Hyde's one time stables)
the building sway, resettle,
the bulldozers haul
on the oil-grimed cable
A mooring and warping
It was almost gentle—
an old craft
in the smallest push of wind—
the dust settle, too
like a pile of coats.

Speculators drum up
vibrations of a past life
(an excuse for a heart-shaped plaque)
and with their destroyer's toys
thump and wallow—
the glutinous mud is infertile—
hippos without
melancholy innuendo.

Nearon

Nearon saw only his sister
at the corner of Hatch
and Lower Leeson Street.
She looked a treat that day
in her shock-white blouse and mini skirt
(You'd never know from here
she was over forty.)

Nearon saw only his sister,
nine years old, he six
she held his hand, said 'Hurry,
Nearon or we'll miss the band
in Stephen's Green.' The camber
slapped the soles of his feet
and the band played Waltzing Matilda.

You Always Have Your Children

You always have your children
they say as though you'd tried
to look a gift-horse in the mouth.
As if you carried this layer
of protection on your back
(an extra layer) unlike the common man.

But your sons blaze brightly
in the bonfire of their youth
while naked as a fish between two banks
you cower between the generations

On your death bed you imagine
you'll raise your head like a gun
your nerve ends quivering
like the needles of a compass
and say you once saw Paul Durcan
at the end of the Western World
making sandcastles for his daughters
and you shouted:

Over to you boy, the inquisition,
the saturnine raven of love.

Michelangelo's David and Me

In the middle was the Renaissance
God the rapacity
In the middle was myself
Anonymous

I confound
This labour of vanity
Method, intention, protestation
The divine molecules
The continuity of marble

My identity quickens
Forty-five in Florence
Fathoms of heat
I am alone

I have been infinitely caused
Compass and clock
I am polymorphous
organised, cornered

This is the city of stone
Called serene
Slow greys
of the Medici Palace
By this stone
Dignity prospers

I strayed in this city
where time has no layers
I have slain Goliath
Am responsible
For Santa Croce

The David's gaze
is anglepoised above my head
The cotton cloth
of a faltering nun
has stroked my calf,
Her robe describes
a rustling circle
a movement of envy
and hunger.

Working Wife's Return

I.
His root is like a horse-radish
and raging in his petticoats
he stalks the garden-god
behind closed blinds.

Darkness everywhere
She gropes around.
She has nothing to give
except the shavings from her head.

She shakes it and the sawdust trembles
in her open brain; smells sweet
as hospitals. While the ever-present
mice hatch numerous plots.

It is dreary scraping the egg yolk
from the table cloth; more vainly dreary
when the jam is mixed with Bartok
and Berlioz and the piano
is clogged with semen.

Dear God, could he not sweep up
in her absence? Then she might consider
a return to his rock-hard socks.

II.
If there were ever anything to shut out
at night
Sigh-like or love or even the stars
to stay bright
even though every crevice is thick with dust.
If there were a welcome to wear away the time.

But just the sledge-hammer of the television
in the interval before the stalk to bed
the armhold of sleep while he raises ructions
reading yesterday's Sunday Times

and then the lean over into the edge of night
the deep ravine of the mattress, sperm matted
fag-filled
the sky-grey sheets wrinkled and pillows
pilloried.

If there were even a few failed snores
to complain about
under the nostrils' quiver,
she'd be the first home like Red Riding Hood
going to her grandmother.

Fantasies and Heroes

Visions like trains
Visions like trains

I shed blood
for a wounded consciousness
like a hungry hippie
on the Himalayas,
for injustice injustices,
Tensing tensing
on the Southern col.
The muscles calling
calling for love
like the raging Ganges.
Red is the river
dead is the taker.
I sell the silk
of Genghis Khan
and gallop away
on a wild white horse
on the Steppes of Mongolia.

Up the steps of the
White House, only
passing through thanks,
thanks to the tea
I've just taken
with S.J. Perelman
and Father So and So, S. J.
on Madison Avenue
have a new one on me
Groucho; O no
I mean Marilyn
Marilyn Monroe.
Please let me share
your shy little pills for

Visions like trains
Visions like trains

We'll ride on the cow-catcher
of the Canadian Pacific
holding the smile of
Buster Keaton
holding the smile
till we get to Moscow

and challenge Kosygin
to a duel with Pushkin,
Lermontov is dying
in the forests of Cuba
and Franz Kafka is waiting
in the groin of the tuba
of Jelly Roll Morton.
And south further south
from the tears of N'Orleans,
under the shadow
of Popocatepetl
I'll never do with Lowry
what he never did.

My blood's in the arrows
of Montezuma
and its cold in the south
and love is howling.
The pemmican's gone,
and the ponies dead.
Captain Oates is out walking
and may be some time
but our snow-blind eyes see

Visions like trains
Visions like trains.

Sally Anne

Sally Anne, Sally Anne
    thin as a tooth pick, Sally Anne
    teased she was and ran from a will o' the wisp
    and married a man with a book of cheques.

Sally Anne, Sally Anne
    looked back once (that was her downfall)
    she was so far away from her feet
    like Alice in Wonderland.

Then they buried Sally Anne
    in a coffin as black as a bowler hat
    but long before the lid was dust
    she'd wormed her way out.

Sally Anne, Sally Anne
    has no plan now—she wings on a jigsaw
    she lies flat on a mat on the floor
    of an unmade bargain.

Sally Anne, is a lazy broad
    she says she's trying to find the other piece
    of sky that was lost like a trick
    but that's a lie.

What will they do with Sally Anne?
    Some people think she's thick
    others say she's a thief and a cheat
    but she's on nobody's conscience which is a relief.

The Adventures of Orpheus and Euridice

I
And Orpheus said
I can't play cache-cache
under the table
for the rest of my life
while Eurydice's puns
couldn't keep up with
Orpheus travelling in front of time.
So she dressed up in a fraction
and waved her tight arse
which she had neatly halved
for the occasion.

The shrinks gathered round
and shook their learned forelocks.
They were dressed in whole numbers
like motor-cycle cops.
(Their faces had come into fashion.)
But they couldn't find her hiding
beneath the piano
while Orpheus composed a new song
called 'I am the last of the romantics
and the last romantic to admit it.'

II
Orpheus' harp sang back at him
so he flipped the coins
and every coin he tossed
fell harps; angry, he hurled
the cash at the barman
who blandly rang the till
'Who am I to Gatsby, who
is he to me,' the barman said.

Meanwhile Eurydice
had sent her brittle pawns

across the enemy lines.
They returned with the news
of a dog with three pink tongues.
'Is that all you have to tell me?'
she said. But the shrinks
who had all turned into chessmen
fell on their sides laughing.
So she ran backwards through the swollen bars
counting the faceless names
for she had so interpreted
their instructions. And the further
back she went, the further
away the sunset. When she arrived
at the hamburger queue, the notice
at the hatch said:
You mustn't get carried away

III
Then Orpheus
entered the depths
as far down as a day's sleep.
He passed the glaziers
the quondam haymakers
on holiday from the Elysian fields
they carried horses
on their shoulders.

He had had the dream
neither cauchemar
white horse, nor reality.

He had followed the river
up the mountain.
Had elbowed out of line
the transient myth.
He had bathed his skin
in the water, and the water
was soft. Soft as folly
played at the end
of a heartstring.

Eurydice was gone now,
gone from the song—
the poem—the steps
down the poem were long
the footfalls on the poem
were as silent as pollen
falling on mushrooms.

He had taken Eurydice's queen,
for the last time
he had dressed in her queen,
her black queen,
her white queen,
he had broken the rules
with bad lines
and false moves.

So he withdrew into time,
and time danced in his favour,
time broke the barriers of doom
and the barriers of light
and numbers.

Whole numbers would come and go
and whole numbers squared
would again square other numbers,
dance numbers, like the island
that dances in the waves,
away beyond the headland
of motor-cycle cops
headshrinkers
beer bottle tops
cigarette butts
half-empty tins.

The army of mice
who play tip and swim
with the well water,
typewriters
that soak up sweat
lost from drinking whiskey.

'Leave your kisses,'
Eurydice had said,
'Hermes is a nice guy
who plays a song called, chase
on a borrowed guitar.'
'Hermes is a secret
and splendid fellow,'

Orpheus had agreed—'Who'll
keep my tears to augment
the waters of Lethe?'

IV

So Eurydice said, 'O.K. Death,
spare the yardstick
and spoil the memory.'
'I'll give you the waters of Lethe,'
Death said, shaking his
Euclidean locks.
'Terror dries the saliva in my mouth,'
she said, 'and I must drink.'
But the pebbles beneath the surface
shone clear like children's faces.

'But you are here to die,'
Death said, laughing.
'It's no laughing matter,' Eurydice said.
Then Orpheus pressed his fingers
into his gloves.
When the splintering mirror
reflected Hermes again
as some kind of angel,
he laughed too.

'Give me the green mountain,'
Orpheus said.

Far Roamed Leto in Travail To See If Any Land Would Be a Dwelling for Her Child

for Jacky

Leto screwed in Paris
within her grey sea
inalienable element.
She lived on garlic
and donkey mince.

There in the screwing
a little calcium was absorbed.
The depth of a nail or
a hollow tooth; tinker
tailor soldier etcetera.
What'll it be a girl or
twins? The sins of ...

She screened her mind like Nijinsky.
In Geneva or Zurich they go
to go mad or die.

She went down the Boul'miche
in the sorrow of her skirt.

C'est ni Communiste ni Catholique
guns and bathos and bad jokes
copied from Prévert.
Later the slogan went
C'est ni Communiste ni Catholique
ni Prévert.

Leto died with Malone
came like a Miro poster
and played the games that Genet
played. In for a penny in for a pound.

But Leto mainly manless
took the painless foetus
to London down Highgate Hill
like Dick Whittington with his bundle.

They hadn't invented the pill
only the telephone and the jungle
and drums beat in her head
like hollow moons.

She resisted Regent's Park
where the hexagonal arses
of business men had smoothed
the benches and allowed Americans
to suck the white motes from her fingernails
till she became as shapeless as a marrow.

Leto waited for the birth of Artemis,
white dancer in the womb.

PART II

Leto's travails are over.
Artemis' spacious dance
fills the horizon.
Pythian Apollo lays his golden blade
beside him.

Hera listens to this intelligence
with cynical ear.
Delos receives you with importunities
and blackmail.

You think you have paid amply for each child
by the circles on your belly;
to make your heart a brass foundry
of noises and shapes.

For every witch a devil; and the
devil you know is better than …

Leto laughs at the thought
of Hera's potential anger.
Some small absurdity of time
is no measure of knowledge
and habit is the shadow of fake …

But Hera has lost her sense of humour
not her power. She bides her time.

Come Sleep in Cancer Ward

Bleached squares of immaculate linen
subside like unmanned parachutes
hard-working hands inquire into the contours of your body
this is a quiet trauma and to be dealt with as such;
they must not find out about the internal rage
that rots inside you like the stump of an old tree killed by frost.
They are so kind, these ministering angels; their hands
are so democratically efficient; herself heedless
of this kindness blames them for they are the nearest to hand
and as with the doctors' intelligent eyes she strains
for their sympathy; saying with hers:
pity me not, for I am intelligent too
the goddess Athene cannot guide me as a woman
for I have journeyed too far on this nightmare voyage
my craft carries too much disloyalty
the men fight in the galleys; their blunt oars
only skirt the fractious waves; the boat describes
an arc and the tiller rasps on the rocks
there's no radar screen to gauge these dangerous rocks
that lurk like killer sharks with blue fins silently
savouring their limitless element;
someone must be blamed or the night won't bring that heavy sleep,
sleep that drags life with claws,
that strains to hold the body
to dream or float in a solid water of silence,
silence that seeps,
that oscillates with its own particular forms
pentagrams like stars—not real stars,

pictures of stars in a planetarium.
The ceiling gets further and further away
recedes in these waves that are moving forms.
There is now a fleet of ships sidling along;
some sort of electric storm has blown up
and the sides of the flotilla are bruised and blasted.

The sea is everywhere now; the sea is the sky,
is beautiful. A rolling darkness upon darkness
time used to have some value, could be divided up

could be pared like a pencil into a fine intensive point
the sea used to be the sea and the sky the sky
then there was a plane a mountain a house
and the houses were divided too; there were lofts
and basements and places with square indentations
where doves went, where doves could sit and make contented
the warmth of their fluffy bodies, a little heat
like a little death beats against human hand
that makes fear; the instinct selects the absolute;
something for the alchemist who turns base metal into gold.

There must be some mistake, allow me to leave, she says,
I have been directed to the wrong place.
It sometimes happens that these mistakes, too,
are made on purpose.
But the doctors have chosen words for this kind of happening;
they have giant tomes and little books
and hippocratic ethics and all sorts of rules
which work perfectly for the golden mien;

Medusa can seek revenge for Perseus; she has broken the mirror,
the kaleidoscopic morsels make pretty remnants;
so natural as they twirl to catch the light
with small respect indeed for such pursuits
as make a cult of bravery
as if bravery were a stage in existence—like youth—
that everyone experiences,

Or she can say she is Nereis, daughter of Neptune
and call it a day.
Lightly lightly drift downward even pretending a little
that she really enjoys the taste of seaweed;
the scraping of bone on crustacea
the rocks full of stinking mortality,
but there are cliffs to be established,
cliffs that rear up like sheets of metal in the skin of a mist
they are luminaries; they have reason and established positions.

They are the almoners who count your money
and make little pencil ticks against varied loss;
they list the guests and slice the thin lemon
into the glasses. It is so perfectly selected,

no room for gatecrashers, for the bums
who steal your possessions and drink your wine.
You must not join in the singing,
make magic like marriage plans,
the honeymoon to be spent in olive groves
where sun and shade are equally divided.
Moreover they are so perfect they will admit mistakes

will disarm you with apologies, explain these things can happen
in this way with the manners of priests
they may momentarily convince you that they understand
and are not an army gone mad from killing.

But their subtlety fails for the occupying army
steals for the sake of stealing; takes the transistor
and fires it into the nearest ditch
for its weight is not worth the carrying.
You have learnt these brand new shining truths
as they dish them out,
you will pass the examination with credits in every colour
and then slip away, evaporate almost before their very eyes,
till your shadow becomes a stain on the wall.
They are sardonically surprised that it could possibly become unclear
unclear like memory that adjusts itself to imagination.

Master Proust himself could hardly better
this situation. You will sink into a glowing nadir
each moment of sensuality a bubble that is isolated
and lives for one fraction of a second before bursting.
There are all sorts of possibilities, like masturbation
or the reading of books about mental health;
the True Way through foods that are organically grown;
dozens of quacks to whet your appetite to re-assure you,
or simply walking to the Holy Land in your stocking feet
or Lourdes or any old place stuffed with tourists,
on quick-way cheap returns as angry and dirty as yourself;

just the same as businessmen in the London underground
who do the same thing every day
with the same discomfort,
because they really believe they're right and you're wrong.

Everybody is born with a ration of strength
which is unvarying in life,
like the length from knee to hoof of a new born colt
that bestraddles the shifting world
complete with defence mechanisms and uncertainty.

There is nothing humble or hopeful in the stance;
you have only been dropped in the grass
for some unknown reason,
it is probably spring and the trees are sleek
with their recurring foliage. There is apple blossom
in other people's gardens.
The universities are spilling over
with beautiful girls and boys with unbelievable hair
and rich mummies and daddies
that somehow never seem to intrude, but supply them
with blank cheques and accounts in Switzers and Brown Thomas.
It used to be possible to have your food delivered
you could ring up the shop
for a pound of spaghetti or a yard of tulle.
Now it turns out
to be a Black Maria
and the police are dunderheads and quite ready
to accept you as a criminal
when you are prepared to say with oriental courtesy
that you are really sorry, will pay back the money even

if it means that your children will go hungry.
You accept the fact that the north is the north
the south the south, that the seagulls come inland
to eat garbage at dawn.

When the streets are empty
save for drunks and office cleaners
—the night watchmen sleep in their little tents—
they have watched right through the night
with nothing in their heads;
for how else, watchmen, could the night be endured—
would you watch the little opening always
for someone who will not come
and share thin shelter against the prevailing winds?
The prevailing wind in the town is your own breathing
that comes blue and sporadic, and if fossilised
would be glorious like parchment.

You have read from the scribe Ani the Book of the Dead
in dyes that were made from mosses and flowers,
your ear has adjusted to the even distribution
of flutes and strings,
and wind out of isolated knowledge makes a musical whole;

the cemetery is neat graves under graves
there is always more room for a corpse,
once consecrated you're home and dried.
If you are rich
you can have a pyramid erected on top of you

or a whole fleet of angels,
designed by someone like Oisín Kelly,
or a sculptor friend of one of the Guinnesses;
the skeleton is not all that vulnerable
and still keeps its human and recognisable contours,
there is absolutely no reason
to confuse it with the bones of a hare
or something other than a creature
with an immortal soul.

Poems in Periodicals
& from Bardwell's Papers

Timor Mortis

After a thin, unwelcome sleep
the bedclothes buckled.
Sheets upholstered on my thighs
The plate-like moon that never seemed to stir
voyeur fictive outside the tempting glass.
I am worn out with waiting
for morning to unstring my tongue

Is it age that has me so unanalysed,
doubting my virility
with which I used to fight the mosquitoes
in my mind?

I remember how sleep once nuzzled me
subdued those dampening, ungendering
doubts, let me down lightly beneath its surface
a warm and hospitable sea to be its sister
patient sibling, wrapped up in its coat

But lately all I seem to hear
is the dividing and subdividing of my cells
as though the red and white corpuscles
waged a mortal war, and I am just a member
of the audience. Sometimes I think
of all those zero-times
the black between one whiskey and the next
the did-I-really-say-that, was it me
and wonder would No Entry be the best

And then be utterly alone
a figure in a fog.

She Laid Her Children at Her Father's Feet

She laid her children
at her father's feet
She gave him their initials
N and M. With lime-white eyes
he stared at them. He said
it's a catechism of disaster
(perhaps he smiled.)

Country Idyll

The Father tees up his golf-ball; he
addresses it, head at half turn
a humorous pull to the left
on a narrow nostril

the mother plumply rigged
splays her fingers round the heavy clump
of hollyhocks and catches the purple
seeded poppy-cup in the lip of her skirt

the puppy skies on its tail
the old cart-horse nods
on his harness—the straddle
string-tied, haphazard, bites the flesh
inviting flies to market in the wound

the long-tailed daughter dimples her Dresden
cheeks; looks at the parents, dead-pan,
her mouth as brazen as a bubble

two smiles loose themselves
like separate space-men in a pewter sky.

Childhood Memory

The thick bark had bled the tree
and the old-cut hay
lay damp in heaps
like mauve sacks.

Meadows of childhood
stack sweet-smelling orchards of goodbyes.
The battered tram
carried us yelling
to curry favour with the hired man:
the child's equivocal position.

My mother, even, would wield
a two-pronged fork
to help yield a good harvest.

The Fly and the Bedbug

(Beaver Row Press, 1984)

Sheila

In her dying she is yet lovely
her silence swings like a sea-plant
at the ocean's edge; the madonna bones
in their cardboard coloured wrappings
make no quiver; yes, secret, she lies
and silent.

Ninety years a spinster—they say
she was rich once—nieces and nephews say—
Hey Sheila! One each side of her, solicitors sit
tearing the hospital cloth
with their ravenous backsides.

Neutered in their defeat,
they have to leave her; her
silence spreads like the snowberries on her island.
She lifts three fingers like a queen,
lets time press on the brows of strangers.
She has returned inland to where
the ponies graze. Sheila! The raspberries drip red
A wisp of wind makes the pippins fall.
She runs to her mother's parsley smelling garden
to hear the gladiolae stiffen.

Mrs Katherine Dunne, Died March 1983

for Macdara Woods

Three on the bottle! Just like me—Kitty—
She gave me a pram then—did she remember?
Now I address her dignity. Summer and winter
on the pavements of time—one day—too
and I cold, she gave me tea as she stood
with snow on her lips and the shyest of smiles.

But that was a while ago and the children
have plagued and played us—s tombola and fife—
The bingo of life picks the strangest numbers
and drums up tunes in the weirdest disarray.

She never would have lived to be incontinent
When the pain came she took a taxi to Sir Patrick
Dun's and lay and waited.
Leaving the street somewhat smaller, the others more garrulous.
When she was there there was no debate
or shallow-handedness. No cavil
nor doubt in her mind that come doleday
I'd always pay her.

In the lamplight of chat—how the country swings
(and not for us) I'd finger the aubergines,
the wounded cabbages, the French Delicious,
tasteless as electricity in their super-shine,
happy to find again an Irish Cox
whose sweet juice runs on the tongue
and she'd say: "Ah—I kept that one for you."

Not easy to be a trader all those years
Summer and winter, watching generations pass
like camels on a video horizon
and stay motionless as Asia, never growing old
herself—just wiser and more beautiful

Was she always waiting for that pain to come
to call a taxi like a tumbril and say "cheerio
and see you soon?" I wonder why I'm left
the simple pride of having known her.

If the Baby Powers we shared
in the rush and tinsel of many Christmas Eves
may not be drunk this year nor any future
year I'll gently hold the gift-horse bridle reins,
wait for the pain to come and call a cab.

Into Madness

for K.M.

If I must go, I must go quickly
to the place where the doors have no handles.
for they have chased me there, branch-men,
buses, teenagers with spikey hair,
chain mail—*dit* Fascist—pardon—maybe it's me.

If I go then, it is to be seen gone, known
to have left—what? The Italian cafe in Fenian Street,
York Street, all the pubs that won't serve me,
or simply the dangers of the past, one circle in my brain
spotlights these to zero—no—maybe it's me
sheltering in my own madness. Is insanity
survival? Or less? An escape from living on the dole,
simply, which, in twenty minutes will be spent on drink?

Please do not stop me, ask me to think
but allow me my special concentration, the spiral of anger
which orchestrates my panic, my stress—a cadenza—
This I must perfect, repeat, to give me time.

The Lady That Went on Strike Against the Early Closing Hours of the Iveagh Hostel

Late of a blue-grained summer night
Lily lay down on her chosen bed—
a God-room on the leaning street.

In Kevin Street Garda station
beset with sleepless blunderings
they covered sheets and sheets of foolscap—
no time for cards or sing-songs round the piano—
from then on it was paper work, paper work.

St Patrick's Cathedral pealed its peals
as far as O'Keefe's the knackers.
Thomas Street raced down to Guinness's.

But Lily, tough-coated Lily
lost in the wonder of closing time
called up a half-one—"And don't forget Agnes"
& when the barman shouted—"Have you no homes to go to?"
Her face was creamed with wily smiles.

They had to thumb through old books,
read old laws, invent new cruelties,
(one fresh-faced young guard suggested
holding her head down the lavatory.)

They got nowhere, seemingly, because
when morning came, Lily was still there—
neatly tucked, umbrella for a roof—
She could sleep in, fine, till Larry opened up.

But every morning Sergeant Mulholland muttered,
"'Tis a damn bloody nuisance."

And Mrs. Mulholland opened the hole in her face
that used to be a mouth
and blew out a few blows of sympathy.

All went ill, went ill, in fact
till the enterprise of nature shot its bolt
and foiled, the force were forced to find
someone else for their daily harassments.
But at least they were able to stop the funeral cortege
from proceeding up Werburgh Street.

For Dermot and Anne-Marie on Attending the Birth of Dallan

Pimlico and Vauxhall Bridge
and that sally port near the Tate
where barges lie deck to deck
like lesbians and Blake
has burnt Satan in Milton's house

Tantalus up to his waist
in the Thames can't drink
though the water leans on his thighs
Pimlico and Eleanor Rigby
at the end of the Chelsea game

Pimlico and splinter city
jostle for life under cranes
"Bow down to the artists
those birds have no wings,
boy, they sing for their supper."

Pimlico and Adam's rib
have put their names on the list
the morainic wastes are groaning
at the end of the map: Come north,
but the compass is spinning

In Pimlico live harlequin
and cat—look fast for the
shadows they leave—citizens stir
in their sleep and Hesperus
sneaks through the grimy window

In Pimlico the lending library lies,
like the hem of cat's hair,
on their pillow—the hazel strand
is the margin of waiting allowed
like the whiskey dream of slow water spreading.

Blackbushe

for Nicholas

She sleeps on the shoulder of the aerodrome
asphalt pits her cheek
pain snaps its teeth;
anticipation has extinguished its plea
too many amateur emotions
have rubbed out the original

But when she wakes to shake off
an acknowledged dream she rouses up
hundreds of smoke-white memories
the dark drums of her past roll over and over

She hears as from another star the speakers
that thunder promises: the dew on the rubbish
will not always be the dirty dress
of the pantomime fairy; dates can be lifted
and set back like starting posts for the sprinters.
There is never only one moon for the madman.

So now at last she watches quietly
while night settles its final business with day.

A million people rise like cattle in an air-raid
Dylan sings

Children's Games

Once upon a time
I saw my two children playing
where Karl Marx was lying
with a tombstone on his head;
they were naked from the waist down

and the English around and around said
Better the children dead
than naked from the waist down

Now I was a foreigner
on that cold Highgate Hill
but I bore no ill to the English
no ill

So I toiled away by the Spaniards
where the English were all lovers
and their legs gleamed O
so cold and naked
naked from the waist down

and I tried another graveyard
and found another plot
where Sigmund Freud was lying
in his eiderdown of weeds

My children, I said, romp away
this little strip is yours
for the dead are mostly idle
and do not care if you are naked
naked from the waist down

and the graves began to smile
and the hymn of England fade
and my children took out their pocket knives
and carved on the limey stone:

Dr Freud lies here in the nettles
we are dancing on his head

The Scattering of the Ashes

for Anna and Bill

I
The grass that's flattened by the orchestra of wind
lies polished for the tenderness of hand,
the stroking of this well-trod shoulder,
not green but yellow and anything but pleasant.
Named downs they lift to the lined horizon,
shrug off the factory town below;
like grey uncarded hair
smoke straggles from the pear-shaped chimneys.

II
And there are seven, connected
by blood or breath, with bowed heads
& gammon cheeks, who falter unevenly in the dried-out ruts
as brother holds brother in a cardboard box;
confused in his own flesh he offers it windward
his fingers ringed by the twine—
It's barely big enough to parcel
an inexpensive clock.
Of what do they chat or whom do they discover
in the this and that of ceremony?

III
Pulverised bone is grey and carbon to the touch,
adheres to palms and the edges of the nails.
As each shakes forth his individual veil,
the wind gusts and divides the matrices;
the immediate matter is settled with the dust
that curious beasts have recently disturbed

IV
Married, long divorced, a couple
in this funeral of chords
unreels a filament of memory.
It's a safe bargaining with the merchandise of years;
the spit-on-the-hand, the luck-penny that's returned.

Berkshire / Dublin 1981

Two Poems in Memoriam Stevie Smith

I

THE GIRL IN A BOX

Once upon a time
There was a girl in a box
And her pretty china face
Was full of love.
        (She never moved.)

Why does she lie there like that
Without moving, so frail, so spent?

Perhaps she is dead, they said
And away they went.

II

DEAR MR PSYCHIATRIST

Dear Mr Psychiatrist
I don't like your pills—
(I prefer my ills.)

I am a doll's house
And my bricks are ruby red.
Mummy and daddy are in my bottles
With pretty plastic phials of love.

O, sweet rainbow, break me.

Two Insect Poems

THE FLY

I am an insect
stuck to the wall
with my wings
transparent
I am an insect
I have no intellect
But I have insight.

If the wall falls
I remain
suspended
If I fall
the wall is solid.
But I shall live
one whole day
with my wings
transparent.

But they will squash me
In time
they will squash me.

They have forgotten
I was useful.

THE BEDBUG

I am a bed bug
I am flat
I am starving

They say God didn't invent me
but I am alive
Society has done for me
I live in a match box

Somebody invented me
(not God)
so I can live indefinitely
in a match-box
alone

I am alive
but they won't feed me
I am transparent
but basically
I am a bed bug.

Office Vignette

Mr. Blank sat on his office stool
dictating to Miss Brazen
the beauties of profit
Miss Brazen took it all down.
"Screw me," she said
when she came to the million pound paragraph.
He did on the edge to edge;
Unscrewed, she resumed her task.
Miss Flower, on the other hand,
the artistic type, couldn't bear it
So much pink flesh on the carpet
So much force against the waste paper basket
So much paper on the floor
and all because of
the high interest rate regime
in the corollary of a falling currency
Mr Blank sat on his office stool
looking at Miss Flower.
He was expecting rain.

Hell's Angels

The metal dancers
have folded their bodies
The music is over.
They have kissed
and made pictures
on the road as rich
as sandstone and
maps of poppy red
and lime-green.

At home the mothers
have folded their bodies
The music is over
Their lips
have not tasted lips
since their children grew.
In the bedroom boredom
of their empty lives
they embrace the gin in the freezer.

Suburban Idyll

The father tees up his golf-ball
he addresses it, head at a half-turn
A humorous pull to the left
of a nervous nostril.

The mother in pumpkin boots
and scarlet neckband splays
her painted fingers round a clump
of heavy seeding hollyhocks

An apronless slut emerges from the kitchen
"Do yez want yer tea," she chants
and the daughter runs to her arms.
She has swung long enough on the love of two strangers

Though two smiles lose themselves
like separate spacemen in a pewter sky.

Has Elizabeth Shaved Her Head?

Has Elizabeth shaved off
her hair; Has Elizabeth
sent it to her

sailor boy? Rock-a-bye
sailor round the rolling
deep; roll my able

bodied man. Is her head
as bald as a question
mark? Is her head

at all lovely now
sailor? Do you want
to bend the sea

with your weight? Dive for the
herring bone weave
on the dark henna

plait? O sailor boy
rock on the rolling
deep for mad Elizabeth

is dead. Do you shock
easily, sailor,
do you shock? For

mad Elizabeth took
the bowls from her
eyes with an iris-stroke

and folded her long
barren body; she folded
up tight like a butterfly

after its life's day's
done. Sailor fill
your vessel, fill it like

a whale and skim skim
the waves like a waltz
Elizabeth does not wait

living; does not cast
her net now, sailor
the coast is clear.

The Limerick graveyard
ticks its tock; morning
opens its silver

mouth; will you dock
easy, now, sailor,
will you dock?

Lullaby

Lullaby sing lullaby
To my sweet baby in his cradle
I'll sing as long as I am able
Your daddy won't come home no more
So I must softly bar the door
Oh lullaby sing lullaby.

Lullaby sing lullaby
To my sweet baby in his cradle
Your mother's voice is growing feeble
Your daddy courts another one
A lass of barely twenty-one
Oh lullaby sing lullaby.

Lullaby sing lullaby
To my sweet baby in his cradle
Your daddy's gone but what is worse
I wish. that I had left him first
Oh lullaby sing lullaby.

The Ballad of the Fisherman's Wife

She brushed the salty weeping from her cheekbones
thrown by the feathered heaving of the spray;
she stubbed her toe against the herring boxes:
death is different; it keeps away

the silver dropped from beaks of flying seagulls;
the swell is rising. Someone ought to say
that harbour symbols cause a crazy freedom
and death is different; it keeps away.

An empty sack! she wandered off
back to her semi-detached along the quay
her rage subsides like over-watered flowers.
Death is different; it keeps away.

Parchment fingers print against the window;
"The boat is late," she whispered, "keep away."
"But I'll come in and prove that nothing alters
death, it's different, it keeps away."

She took the 'Foreign Missions' from the dresser
She took a fiver out of last week's pay
"Bring bread and wine and spirits, then," she ordered.
"Death is different, it keeps away."

Lobster Fishing

Lend me your education,
glum Clare-man
while your sockless boots
slide on the algae.

Under the jaw-bone of cliff
whipped by the anxious sleeves of wind
the night air burns with salt.
The cliffs shout back at the sea,
their gun-metal mouths are hungry
for lacy meetings.

We have eased ourselves down,
promoted the cliff-stairs to safe passage.
Above the sea-howl each step
widening on to the outcrop of armoured rock
makes its individual sound as the sea-plants crack.
"Beach the bloody crates!"

Orders is orders
for he is no crazy man; pots are expensive,
a living must be got.
His anger swings in the storm like a metal moon
no caution allowed
in these recondite surroundings.

It was fighting for hours, it seemed,
the wet ropes rasping already frozen fingers
till crowding back on the baize shelves of Kilbaha
The crates are counted. Six, all safe—
he is exultant. The ocean swell behind us,
we'll go to Kilrush and later cash the cheque.

Yet for me, when the thin line of dawn
splinters the kitchen window
I am conscious of a poor green thing
too small to sell and ready for the pot.

I should much prefer to tie it on a string
and prance upon a street
mindful of Gérard de Nerval.

I'll Do the Messages

To Edward and John

I'll do the messages,
give me the poison drops
from the orphan's tongue
I'll pre-digest the wrong;

I'll sell the flags for the flag-seller
and hold the tiresome horse
for the smith with four dead wives.

The apple is in your side, my brother
I'll learn the Blue Danube
from the village dressmaker,
I am the scapegoat and I'll dance
to someone else's tune.

Ten tall sunflowers grew in my garden.
They played the incomparable artist's game:
one black eye each and a dart
that was the start of my garden.

I walked through the trees of adolescence
the angry walnut and sheltering beech.
A seed was sown in an ebony heart
let the bud decide where the flower shall fall.

Megan Fair 1977 Remembered

Cross-legged, she sits, the pregnant one
her boyfriend beside her, the flame of pride
illuminates the cushion of his cheeks.
My sons throw frisbee beyond the circle of the camp—
a white knife skimming the shoulder of the field—
My daughter bends from me to whisper to the embers;
I finger the back of her hair. Rising and falling
against the fire it is darker than fire—
the colour of drenched apricot.
It ribs against my palm,
nervous, electric, compelling.

In a pit we have made this fire,
scooped the crusted earth with our fingers
and laid criss-cross the twigs
ignited by sandwich wrappings, old newspaper
till the bronze flame entered the sides of the logs
and it was comfortable, would work for us,
make the grass a shade warmer for our thighs,
the skin tighten on our cheeks.

The children are fed first; my daughter
has spread the cloth way back from the heat;
they are everywhere like dark squirrels
cupping their hands for the offerings she has to give.
Already the black pot bubbles—the soup slides quietly
up the edges. Her limbs are loose and purposeful;
her thoughts retain their cosmic pattern.

Now the fires are everywhere in the horn of night.
For a long time it was twilight,
a muslin of mist had clothed the landscape
but now the clusters of distant Lowry figures—
all at business with life—
are at work kindling carefully as we did,
stitching rubies to the flank of the secret hill.

There is nothing to do now only wait
for the acres of feeling to be ploughed back into time—
a brief memory of others perhaps, the solid footsteps of strangers
the Welsh, curious as bullocks, about this Irish family
or what we are wary of in the valley, hidden below—
a suspicious village, a chapel crouching in its bed of meadowsweet
or the offering of the wine of oak-leaves and mountain ash.

Rooms

The old man dead. Sounds
from the kitchen. The hands,
enormous, loosely crossed.
The flesh still brown. An
out-of-doors man. The cheeks
two yellow bowls. Eyes shut.

Everything very clean and trim.
the son stands in the doorway
the daughter, an empty woman
near the bed, bends over slightly
touches the sheet, the bolster,
meets the son's eyes. Then
touches the old man's wrist
with her index finger.

In the kitchen they stand up
with tea-cups in their hands;
the wife alone
is active. The wind
snuffles under the back door
and lifts the calendar
from the wall.

The two nuns in the drawing-room
as prim as hat-pins have
been told to wait. The logs
whisper—a cinder falls—a hand—
an enormous hand—picks up
the brass fire-tongs.

Lines for My Father

After the furnace had subsided. “Still,
it was a mortal blaze,” they said
“Mahogany and sycamore and oak,”
“The Liffey itself could not have quenched the flames.”
Then someone kicked the smouldering remains,
“The fire-brigade was something of a joke.”
There was nothing left but fretful wisps of smoke.
He said: “If you do that you’ll burn your boots as well.”

> On the eve of my geography exam
> he took me to the Magic Flute
> There at the booking office, I remonstrated
> “I know no geography, I ought to be at home”
> To hell with geography, he stated.

The distant murmur of the waterfall
the salmon’s undersides are silver in the sun,
they rest exhausted, then they try again,
the bog-fed Liffey waters push
them back and back. Lax—hlaup. It is suggested
the great scourge Thorkil wandered there
and marvelled at the efforts of the fish.

> In Leixlip house the piano stool
> stood firm, Victorian and worn,
> while outside was Georgian symmetry
> of granite, carted stone by stone.
> with wicket-keepers broken fingers
> he played Leoncavallo, but expertly
> I sang (who could hardly be called a singer)
> On with the motley . . .

Confey

In the torn and dirty sheets of those winter years,
spent in my wet mac, clutching the green packet
with its fiery orange sash—four Woodbines!—
and my mongrel dog scratching its pedigree of fleas,
I was happy as a child can be, hiding under the shelf of Confey.

Drunk from the spilling rain the stumpy field
shrank from the ruined church, the glue factory—
Four headstones, I remember, aslant and faceless as winos.

The winter mists came early then,
Tucked up the river in a long white scarf
while heavy with fish and water hens
it rolled on quietly through the textured night

Two pence ha'penny—old money—
not much to pay in retrospect
for an imaginary summer that someday I might sing.

We Don’t Serve Travelling People

The barman attacks the counter—
his dry cloth bolting in fury
along the plastic beam.
His eyes like electric studs
fasten on to me—
I feel the familiar pain.

We don’t serve travelling people
or prostitutes.

No, I am not popular in pubs—
nine out of ten times I hear
that icy ‘madam’ cast up on the shore
of my uncomplaining retreat.
Not here, not there—from Liffey Street
to Donnybrook and back—
Only in Grogan’s or The Sword
can I rest the prostitution
of my weary but travelling mind.

In My Darling Liza's Eyes

for Jacky

In my darling Liza's eyes
I see her father
Her shoulders are square like his
as though she carried two buckets
on a yoke

She leans over the bar and slurps her vodka
Oh Liza, do you hear that voice in your throat?

Moving House

The house unfolds and straightens
with relief. We've discarded the stone, the elephant,
the Japanese parasol and the pile
of unfinished poems
—they are like rotten fruit—
(might be a core worth extracting.)

Are you taking the piano?—Yes
the mice are nesting in the keys
and sit with paws crossed like expectant choirboys.

We are tired of this move
and all the other moves we've made
and tired of the people who are tired
of carting memories around.

The magic of summer took us by the neck
and wrung us out like an old sock
is it possible we've accumulated
so much rubbish in so short a time?

Let us go then quickly before dark
in this way we'll close the shutters of absence
and find a new set of trivia and attachments

We Sell You Buy

We sell, you buy,
Exocet, Pershing, Cruise, what odds?
We sell, you buy.

We have reasons aplenty, piled up like pillows
on the creaking bed of your desire
to see the earth crack like an egg
and pour itself into the empty cup of space.
We sell, you buy.

The world's on the H.P. spiral
if we make black snow we must distribute.
Sales distribution, input, output,
that's the name of the game.

Why can't you understand, you of feeble
belief "That man can't possibly do this"?
Of course you'll purchase the brand new sun
that'll give you a tan without flying south
For the price you're prepared to give—
freedom was the word I think you
mentioned?

I once read a book about some old Jap
who saw the shadow of his daughter on a wall
by the corkscrew of fate he survived to tell the tale,
went far away and cultivated carp.

Options

for Siobhan, Fiona, Rita, Sinead

"You for the 'ostel, luv,
'ere...." She wanders off
through the iron buttress of Victoria Station
her heavy bag the lesser incumbrance—
Westcliffe Road, number thirty-two? Thirty-two!
The sum of twice her age.

"You've left it too late,"
the Indian doctor says—"four months, a risk
I cannot take."
As the needle of this information
scratches her childish brain
she sees her future dulled, her life destroyed
The option: a furnished room in Dublin 6
the dole of twenty-eight a week
or here in Westcliffe Road for five months flat.

O happy happy men and creepy females
who speak of a 'Caring Society'
with acid on their lips.

Ferdinand

FERDINAND LIVES

Ferdinand lives—excelsior!
        Spring has come, summer is
        round the corner.
        Ferdinand has left his bed
        & holds a bud in his left hand.

"That's my bud, Ferdinand,
        I got it first."
        Some whipper-snapper
        of a costing clerk, was Ferdinand once—
        if Ferdinand never adjusted
        to the mores of modern fat-cattery
        he may not be entirely blamed,
        "The buds are for everyone," he says.
        "Not so, Ferdinand, don't fool yourself."

"O.K. then, Ferdinand, go back to bed,"
        he says to himself.
        "Go back to your black bed and scratch your sores
        your children are walking the roads;
        they are no more enlightened
        for the cudgel of your outdated idealism."

FERDINAND REMEMBERS HIS RESPONSIBILITIES

Four times a father, Ferdinand's sons
prey heavily on his mind.
Ferdinand erect, clean, indignant,
attends the parents' meeting.
His questions falter—feeble whisperings
fail to catch the chairman's world-wise ears.
His worst fears are realised.

"You are rat-repulsive, Ferdinand—
remain invisible—your suggestions are redundant—
have no bearing on the rush and gathering

of daily life as seen by the majority."
Such faultless logic wraps up Ferdinand's heart
in its cold wet glove—he quails.

"Where are you, my sons, now?"
Ferdinand groans. "All the best orchards
robbed, all locks picked."
The headmaster pierces him with his withering sword.
Without a further mutter, he slinks home
to the dirty eiderdown of his eternal poverty,
his collar drenched in tears
to kiss the faces of his sons
in the mirror; lips against furtive lips.
"My four boys of flesh are nescient
of this fibrous bundle—must go forth,
fake up new logic—exert, like Sisyphus,
mad strength for useless tasks—
undo and do all knots with feverish gaiety."

FERDINAND ROMANTIC

A mania for happiness has Ferdinand.
Hope, springing eternal, he potters drily
through London squares, back alleys and pock-marked
houses of Pimlico. Tired Ferdinand leans
by the eighteen bus stop; mazed in wonder
he searches Notting Hill Gate and other
vortices of grey Victoriana
for glimpses of Ferdinand young, winsome
and strong as a beaver; loved 'em
left 'em once, thought Ferdinand, exhaustion—
insulated. "Who are all these suited
publishers who take dinner by candle-flame.
Name one!" cried he, silently, "Who'll
meet sad Ferdinand's eye and pass the time of day."
Ferdinand, drunk in Bloomsbury shunts
back and forth in the mill of happy English
city-skaters. "Who'll buy my pretty wares,
my fruit, my seedless pomegranates?" His ankles swell
as the bar recedes. In the ding-dong
closing hours of the afternoon
he confronts the post-meridian sun.

Must he choose to lie beneath blankets
whose turf-like surface will scrape his pearly skin
in some back street doss when Maries and
Katherines once vied noisily
for his mystical fondlings in their beds?

"Ach Jesus," he says, "lies—all lies
your mutton-face was never anyone's dream
yet somewhere down the line you were keen as a star
in the exalted planetarium of love."

Shedding the petals thus on the stain
of his present earthly state, he whines
to Euston's crystalline waste
to be carted fitfully back; this latest upset
locked in his chest. "Best be reasonable,"
he mutters. "At least you had the wit
to purchase the return ticket
of your great humiliation."

FERDINAND DREAMS

Ferdinand sits at a grand table.
On his lap, the paper napkin lies—
He hails the waiter.
"O, dog-like and dutiful, kneel!"
Humble petitioner as is he who serves,
joins in steeple-prayer two indices.

Ferdinand, with wine in head and hand
pours joyfully to bless the waiter's nape
and waves the waiter to his feet.
"O, servant, rise, and in future
do not act the maggot . . ."

Now, fast friends, they are
in conspiratorial love
they hold hands sometimes and share the same fork
(as fast friends should) and when
they fluff the same white roll of bread,
pop cotton pillules into each other's mouths
and laugh with the same insouciance.

FERDINAND HILARIOUS

At last Ferdinand is dead.
His laughter, the most infectious
breezes through the newly nurtured grass
that some pathetic wellwisher
has planted on his grave.

He sits among old friends,
drinks champagne and celebrates
his majestic intellect.
"I always stole from the rich
and gave to the indigent,
preserved a frank and open nature,"
Ferdinand says. "And have conversed
with shadowy illusions of fame and fiscal stability."
Such claims to reason, his friends think
unseemly and urge him to drink up.

Ferdinand rapidly demolishes several magnums,
asserts his right to fantasy—now well dead
All should be left to his decisions and Ferdinand laughs
so happily that his friends share this opiate
as if distinguished strangers were present.

Prison Poems

I
Old prison doors are solid;
of seasoned oak, pitch-pine or teak,
satisfactorily planned with doors
within doors—small rectilinear slits,
spy-holes, gratings.
The whole, uneven as plaited silk and printed
with dead-hand grease like the decks
of old sea-going vessels.

Yes, old prison doors, they say, are
ineluctable necessities and those
who slouch around like turtles
must marvel at the judges in their belvederes
who sing from above melodious panegyrics
to morality and its usages.

They sometimes tender fancifully that 'Life'
is far too short a sentence.

Life is a very short word.

II
Dawn lifts its blue-veined face
        slaps the chimney, slides down,
        disappears beyond the kitchens.

Seagulls, fulmars, kittiwakes
        freewheel for a frenzied dive.

Dawn has spoken, has cried
        Kyow, kyow, kyawk.

Day shakes out its dirty shirt;
        sleeves whisper, "They've sold us down the river."

Afternoon half rises, inert, polite.
        It soon is left for dead.

Night straps down its quilt
        Forces the colours behind our eyes.

We believe!
        Like children believe
        in the tall words of their picture books.

III *(For Pat McCann)*
I walk the crazy paving, the path of lies
the micro-chip of satisfaction
and mingle with the funny-money men
who gossip on the shoulder of the judges.
But I think of you between the intervals of pacing
or silence as on the edge of circumstance

and with twice and nothing of what they have,
the bastards.

I send you the white bird of attendance,
the swallow that left too soon, migrated south,
the simplicities of daisies under boots.

Faithful to *Dallas*, the dishwater of the box,
those men are keenly anxious about the future of J.R.
plaiting their egos round each others' throats,
their rightful help to riches, their belief

Remember Jean-Paul Sartre and other soldiers of fortune
who lived on the rim of existence and survived;
the cinder that drops beneath the grate and stays alight,
the fish that lies beneath the shadow of a stone.

IV
I do so want to live but my body
stringent in its monkey-martyrdom
withdraws into shadow-splendour.
It knows I am helpless now to order it.

In effect, the delay in dying spreads
flat and reflective as a mirror.
Voices of others at one remove
deploy old friends, natives of my mind.
They argue, frustrate me with their insistence.

It's hard to see; motes of light tumble
like tadpoles; I remember chemistry,
a cross teacher, the jargon of formulae
how all could be clarified in the body-mortal
if only I paid attention.

Some days I am careless; I cope adequately
with skin and thighs. Feet, more determined
claim my attention as though
they braved the frontier without permit.
This amuses me; I admire them for their stress
of personality. I allow them to peer from beneath
their triangle of blanket; I would like to meet them half-way,
acknowledge that their geometry is relevant.

On other days I am invaded by heat, bothered
by the mass of bone, my skull, especially.
In this state my mind is laid back
for the repeated information of pain.

I do so want to live or is that someone else talking?

V

This way madam! Miss, Mrs, Ms. It's all the same
in the darkened corridor, in the elbow of orange light
shed by the penitentiary bulb.

She even feels a seam of pity
for the unhappy puzzle of the young cop's face
but she knows she could peddle the flowers of friendship
till the cows went home and she'd only learn one fact:
he hates her.

For this is the way of things;
not only is she in the wrong, she is a woman.
The tremble of God's eyelid wouldn't open
or storm the Bastille of his mind.
How has he sunk so low as to have to walk
with such an evil thing?

Her own identity is something left behind
with generous other days on dirty Dublin streets
like watching the sad expression on her landlord's face
or fixing the meter quickly before it's read
or even a morning queuing for the dole.

But the crash of the heavy lock resounds;
the childhood mortice of an unknown room
and she is again a child on whom fleshless silence
clamps its morbid teeth.

She lies under the weight of it
in the air that's as cold as salt and with her stare
breaks up the surface of the cobbled wall
beneath whose cloak of dust, graffiti, blood,
a million creatures whisper; with or without her
their parliament is never still.

Poems in Periodicals
& from Bardwell's Papers

Poems in Memoriam Stevie Smyth

USELESS GHOST

I am a ghost
with two chains round my ankles
(it's thankless being this kind of ghost
clanking all over the house
when everyone could be sleeping)

What are you doing, ghost,
keeping the whole house awake
are there not some kind of pills
that a ghost like you could take?

No, ghost, we think you're on the wrong tack
It's not that we're afraid of you,
no, you needn't imagine that,
it's just that you clatter about like a bad dose

There's places for your type of ghost
where they lock you up tight
and you'd never again disturb our sleep
though you haunted with all your might.

THE PARADOX OF THE MORNING RIDER

I love to go riding in the park
on a bright summer morning
where the grass is green and sweet
and the rooks are cawing
but o, what an unhappy thing it is
riding in the part that says 'no riding'
someone went that way long ago
and death came sliding
through the sweet summer grass
o, it wasn't nice of him to do that
it wasn't kind of him at all
for he is greasy and fat
and not at all sensitive
his business is to keep you alive.

Conversation

I have come to evict you
and your husband
I have no husband
The paper says Mr and Mrs X
There is no Mr X
But you and your husband must get out
I have no husband
I am the Sheriff
I have my instructions
I know you're the Sheriff
With your instructions
I came on my Honda 50
I saw you ride in
This is very irregular
But quite usual
You and your husband must leave now
I already told you
It says here . . .
I know it says.
You don't have a husband?
Yes I mean No.
So I don't have to leave?
Here are the papers
I don't want the papers
Are any of these people your husband?
No. This is an eviction party.

Chauffeur

There are islands of the mind
thin as a head's hair
embarrassingly different
uninterested
in the mind's sea-runner

Be my chauffeur
but don't ask me to dinner

Now the wind gathers
howls in its awkward way
breaks down
kneels, says prayers
to the uncompromising
universe, tortures

Be my chauffeur
but don't ask me to dinner

And there are others
who went
sold up, pulled stakes
decided

I cannot decide
I am beyond decision
the whole showing
is false

Be my chauffeur
but don't ask me to dinner

Outside the Dispensary

Recalling that God made the Sphinx
and he and the devil between them Edward Dahlberg
and the Tahitian cannibals invented the tenderiser
I queue for vitamins outside the dispensary
in the Coombe
What quirk of vanity
distorts my faculties
as perished with the cold
I'm up to my knees in melting snow
my feet either wet, frozen or amputated

My hands dead from the wrist downwards
great globules of slush slaver down
my neck and between my breasts

But my case is not the worst
not by a long chalk
what about that old woman with three coats
doubled in two like an N

that red-eyed wheezing ancient
tear ducts blocked, voice gone to a croak
that tubercular baby, with the spastic brother
What about them. Or the coeliac dwarf
or the teenage beauty with withered legs

What balsam, pillule, bottle,
what tiny phial,
will empty the blocked arteries
loosen the cleft palate.

The black rose withers in the snow
and all the daft and aged are cheating
Death. I, among you, salute you
and I envy you your facility
I'll bequeath you my Dahlberg and my Borges
if you grant me back a moiety
of what I flogged long ago

Fathers

Was one Oscar, whose
crystal fingers made
her blood rush in the station yard?

Did she swim with Brian
beyond her breath
and lie up in a beach in Scotland?

Or did Finton feather
his nest with a goose quill
that wrote like an Arab?

Fathers came easy
pestle and mortar
and she was a slow pigeon

who jumped too late
on the tarmac before the screech
of the vulcanised wheel

Yet her sons' smiles humour her
they are the rays of the sun come to Calary
to strip the blankets off the hills

And there is also
the chestnut girl prancing
her boots alone
would bring moonluck and sunstars

She is dancing Artemis
golden hunter girl.

Marlene Dietrich

The Dutch woman
watching the telly
said she had three
body-lifts, face-lifts
galore.

Great gravel voiced woman
how they hate you
They forget to ask the lads
in the back of Mooney's
what they're having,
to call their orders.

Sister save yourself
from the vultures
of jealousy
If age cracks the artifice
of your undoubted beauty
just tell 'em you're having the same.

Paris

Last year the changeling
of time was my flintstone—
airport Charles de Gaulle
in the fret and fume
of diesel and expensive coffee
the cut of thirty years or so
to the steps at Calais

sun and jeans and berets
boats like tricks and crates
the plump sea swelling
with some indifference.
But last year it was love
and pain and running blood
exchanged the fusty green
and drumlin claustro-madness
booze, debunked
like a kid escaped from school.

Two lovers—myself, the city
entwined in heat and desperation
flailing their arms, octopi
fighting the swordfish
fighting back.

That House

She dreamt always
of getting that house,
that house with the lucky break
that house in the right place
at the right time.

But she never knew
a right time or place
Although
once she owned
a wheelbarrow.

Cancer

That woman knew
she had cancer.
No one else knew it,
neither doctor nor nun
but she knew it.

She knew by the crab's claws
she ate at the harbour
she knew it well
that crab, that young crab
growing and growing
as though growing was all
it could do.

One day she said
to the the infirmary porter
who was passing on his bike,
"Hey you, I've got cancer
I've got cancer in my gut."
"Where?" He shouted
into an oncoming bus.

So they scrubbed
the cancer table
in the infirmary
it was blue-clean

and

"It's somewhere down
the last half mile,"
was the last thing
she said.

from

The White Beach

(Salmon Poetry, 1998)

*

eighties

He Tries to Understand But Cannot

He tries to understand but cannot
how writing books means lots and lots of time
away from him. He loves her for
the little marks she makes on paper,
shouts his approval in every bar in town.
But when he sees her sitting at her desk
he wants to kill her.
He tries and tries but cannot understand.

One day he came home rotten drunk
and screaming, Where the fuck's my dinner?
He yelled so loud the neighbours came
but he was strong and they were weak,
they ran.

He tries to understand but cannot.
It is beyond him how at first he loved her
for the little marks on paper that she made
but didn't realise how come they got there,
that sometimes she must sit and write them down.

Alas this story has no ending.
Eventually he'll kill her, that she knows.
With slender hands he'll throttle her
and boast about her writings in the town.

Spring Song

O the lacuna of spring—
flowers, sun, buds, birds nesting.
But in my mirror peers Ms Death—
Meat face, she is.
But O the lacuna of spring.

It's a long street this death.
I see my grandfather walking his Fido
'Come along, little doggie, come along.'

Grandpa died in '52
and he is walking the street of my death
with his Fido.

He says 'what a queer life you lead as a poet'.
He doesn't call me a poetess
because he has learnt in his deathness
that Sappho started the game—
Sappho of so many lovers
all as pretty as butterflies
and she was a poet.

The tom cat has left his spoor.
It smells of grapefruit in the early morning kitchen.
New life! New life! New lives for old.
(When I was a lass I also waited in the market place
but no one told me how to rub the lamp.)

However I salute the fathers of my children
though nary a one could care
that in this spring of my ancient years
I type by the cat house:
Oh, the lacuna of spring.

The Flight

The flight was inevitable
(she couldn't remember much
except she wound up in a grotto).
Somewhere in the blue light
a statue was there—water
also was involved—
it made a curious noise
like small feet running
and she was sick—eclipsed
in a venom of nausea.

The vomit kept coming
excluding breath as though her lungs
were parcelled up against her throat.

There was a rocking sound
of some coarse music in her head
each pain had its own gender
taking in turn its male or female form,
making sport of her own child's body.

She felt she could hear the grass growing,
the growling of stones
or feel the tilt of the earth
as it tried to shoulder her off.
Sometimes she knelt or squatted.
As dawn ventured would have made a weird triangle
(had anyone seen her).

But of course, the one person
on whose door she knocked,
half-dressed, be-slippered,
soutane-less, certainly Godless
didn't want to know, so did not see.

Sometimes the earth may give a jerk,
when all the creatures communicate;
there may be a hint of cows
the bleat of a January lamb
the birth of another unwanted baby
the death of a girl and her child.

I'm Trying To Tell You, Mr Justice Lynch

i.m. The Kerry Babies Tribunal

My feet drag, it is my seventh month
and eyes, all eyes my enemies.
I must be furtive, sly
as if to hide the pumping heart
of a stolen bird. (My bird,
that other, flies further to the horizon.
Can I ride you now
like the wren on the eagle's back,
let the sun scorch my wings?
There is no quiet breath
for my wind-blown feathers
to make my white skin glow.)

The bird pants—each
his own calendar—each his own first
fretful step into an unknown
inquisition—to die or live
without a dream—without a story
for each should have his tale eventually.

So when my time is come
I will stand in the sour grass
of a long gone summer
and, with the first cry, see
my rivers snake the scutch
as red is to black in an April's dawn.

St Brigid's Day 1989

The women's calls
go up across the lake.
On this still day their voices
whip the air—staccato notes
behind the reed-hushed margin.

Winter is writing out its past
before its time
while they trail the shore
anxious to garner reeds
for Brigid's Cross, bending
in all their different flesh-shapes
like shoppers to admire a bud,
an early primrose, a robin
shrilly calling to its mate.

Although I gather rushes
like these strolling women
I'm made conscious
of the decades that divide us
and that I should be celebrating
Brigid in her strength
of fruitfulness and learning.

I can only offer her the satchel of these years,
I too, will make a cross, for luck and irony.
Amongst the witches' coven I will raise my glass
so my children's children's children
will gather rushes for her turning.

Don’t Go Down That Road

for John McLachlan

John said, as sons will,
with some concern and disapproval,
Don’t go down that road.

A Christmas of tinsel and turmoil,
it was, until
the year split like an envelope,
and opened the wounds—
a half-plucked pheasant,
the turkey carcass like a rusting car.

Oh my God, are the rocks
grinding themselves to powder
are the scars screaming their pain
to the wind to cut them clean.

An old man feeds his bullocks,
knee deep in Monaghan mud,
hocks, splashed, joints
locked in anticipation.
Life goes on, they say,
willy-nilly, as though you could toss
the earth like a coin
and it didn’t matter how it fell.

But I had gone down that road
of ivy and torn dreams,
my children around me—men and women—
nervous of me and arrogant as stars,
knowing that I’d disgrace them once again.

He said, I shouldn’t have gone that road,
but I didn’t listen, O, I didn’t listen.

Dostoevsky's Grave

(Dedalus Press, 1991)

Obituary for Leland Bardwell

Lea – land – there was no shelter there;
no shelter from the cutting North.
So she went North into the brume.
For a while the new broom swept clean
but then the ashes of her bed
soon turned to rust.
And there was cold.
The earth was a frozen lump.
North again she went into the further
doom where the map ends
and she remembered the South
where the strollers were
like Mandarin figures on a Chinese silk;
"Have I come too far?" she asked
an old man making masks.
But he was waspish and unkind;
he answered not but pointed with skinny hand
to Lea – land – there was no shelter there.

Housewife

They filled in the halo
with chalk
a better picture, this,
they thought
(for she's no saint.)
They put pebbles on her nipples
to weigh them down.

She feigned patience;
she waited,
    waited,
        waited.

Occasionally, during the waiting period
she came up with a small truth
while sweeping the dust
off the bread; at first
there was fruit, and left-overs
to finish up; soon
the water even was gone,
and money was everything.

Then the panther came
and sat on her lap.
His paws created a diversion
as soft as mushrooms on her thighs.

They tried to send her away
but she sat still.
(They knew there'd be a toll
for her returning)
But that would be later
much later.

She was crouching now,
her breasts lay naked on her ribs
like cotton gloves,

her legs had got like daffodil stalks
but her eyes were still angry.

The panther had gone,

The only way she knew this
was by the tone of their voices.

The way they could tell she was still there
was by the noise of the cupboard doors
being opened and shut.
She must be looking for something
they said.

Sailor Song

i.m. Commander Robert Cooper

My great uncle Bob went French
and spoke of *Naufrages*
—he had traded sailors like silk
in foreign parts.
He showed me "Beetlejuice"
the brightest of all Orion's mates.

The night sky spins on the lever
the mariners love—it's a nervous sea
The Leeward Islands lift and dip
the sailors are braced by a nip of rum.
Is it spikenard that wafts through the smothering fog?
(The seabed lifts as the cormorants dive.)

With the drift of years the waves
must have arched their backs to flatter
the sailor who scanned his vegetable plot,
the furcoated caterpillar swung
on the cabbage leaf.
(The Red Admiral pinned to the box
was a butterfly hoax.)
It was strange that an old old man should have jet black hair.

I feared that he would fall or drop
a priceless porcelain jar—I feared
he would trip on the crusty stair
and a carved wood head would bounce and chip
but I never feared that he would die.

Only part of the heart's equipped
for a legacy of empty rooms—
a telescope to read the sky,
the lingering camphor smell
in the empty butterfly box.

Husbands

My first husband hated intelligent women
he thought they were like avocado pears,
expensive, tasteless.

He said if I was let loose
I might go to Mexico
although his horizons
were leather skirts.

My second husband hated Mexicans
and me. He said we had ended the transfer.
He liked Antonioni women
with short hair and big bums
and wanted to be one.

I'd like a new one with no hatreds
and superb teeth
Both my husbands had grey smiles
and were transvestites.

I thought that stupid
(so what if my breasts
are like two fried eggs?)
They haven't any.

I was once screwed in Euston Station
and saw mercury running.
If I could have bottled it
I'd have made a fortune.

On Being Shut out of Desmond O'Grady's Flat in the Small Hours

Was it for this we crossed the Rubicon
(the crazy monk on roller skates)
Dove la scuola Athenaeum?
(A thousand Japs in the Vatican)

Amor dapis means amor lacrimarum
Legal organic high—
(There are nettles by the Tiber
they are wet, they sting.)
Non sunt fiori
And thou shalt weep
upon the water.

With the small annoyances of dawn—
a lost key—
il Professore sleeps
with his halo askew.

We'll play peripheral giants
and tell half the story

Wife Waits for Husband

Why do you come wine-dressed
with your whisky kisses
and throw back my curtain
wanting my ripples?

I do not lie corsetted
there is no toll-gate
come crazy come weary
but do not come wine-dressed
with your whisky kisses

turn over tiredly turn
the bed over
tell me I'm whoring
tell me I'm wrong
but don't come with
tresses don't come with weeds
the dandelion clock
is the maker of seeds

he loves me he loves me
he loves me not lately

but do not come wine-dressed
from botchy night glories
do not come wine-dressed
with mother made stories

come with the whisky
and give me to drink
the future is fox-glove
it's poison it's poison
but poppy will soften
the lines on my street.

Inishbofin

Mikey's eyes see further than the long sea
  in the short bar.
If an island is another land it isn't Ireland
and the islanders' insulated laugh is a valediction
  that no partings fathom.

Yet we return again and again
  as the pleated sea swells
to allow ourselves that moment of joy
as the Melody docks, the crafty old engines
  grinding to a halt
And Mikey's cagey welcome, small drops of merriment
  waltzing in the irises
would make the twelve bens bow down in salutation.

His brother Christy rests athwart the bows
  (he never smiles)
His salt lips are dried by his daily death
  banging from port to port with cargo and caution
His melody is the song he sings when the sun
  dips over the island's spine.

The rest of the crew, Young Jim, in his forty years
  a stranger to both, harbours his eyes
  like the skin of the bog where the sun runs like a scythe,
languid and orderly in his labour he hurls
  the Guinness kegs on the harbour tip
Short shrift for the returning vagrants
  from Kensal Rise or Ealing West
or the Johnnie-come-latelies like ourselves
  gratefully settled like plovers on motionless ground
while the crowd disperses and the island, a figure of eight
subsides once more in its ocean bed.

Mikey, stately in his sixty years
drifts to Day's Bar, leaving the future behind him.

An Afternoon with the Artist at The Quinn Club

for Gerry Mangan

Pat Quinn is the plenipotentiary
of compassion—like the blue whale
he puffs and gurgles—gurgles and puffs
while the cloves of hot spirit
cluster his lips he spreads vines
on the tampered marrow-skin
the monastery of his seventh child.

The dusk made a twist of lemon in a furtive sky
damp winter settled on the Wicklow night
sealed the little episodes of mud
with slate thin ice—the children repaired
with effortless confusion
to the thud of the pin-ball tables.

Free mandarin roots for all
roll up somnambulists, the empire is yours
we are the great sharers
something for all the family.
The ticket man has braced his varicose heart
has adopted a surgeon's smile
He knows the camels of fortune
don't come to poets. When the knees
swell and mottle like turnips
they'll yell for the knife.

The artist drinks his vodka straight—
we toast—all centuries combine—
the supreme and wide dominion—
the year of the Tiger.

We listen carefully to the cushions.

Inishbofin (the Roue)

In the hot roar of Murray's bar
the roue stares lustfully
the old trench-coat hardened
like asbestos
—catch as catch can—
on the way to the toilet

We're crazy about this place
of wild mint and garlic
imagine poems can solve everything
grow into the landscape
like the surface turf
or like adding polish to a shoe

But the roue is there
sanding his lust in the blind way
we trip in ruts on a moonless night
if he goes home empty
with his limping dog
we lie untouched
among the nameless grave stones.

Mother Said it Would Be All Right When Frances Came

Mother said it would be all right
when Frances came

Since the consumption took Rose
those roses on her cheeks,
mother said, meant T.B.

But it would be all right
when Frances came

And those fungi
camping in corners
and the case of the dead bat
in the meat safe
yes it would be all right
when Frances came.

Mother said, we must impress Frances
clean up the kitchen, make all ship shape
so I dressed up like All Hallows Eve
and Frances came.

She came and swept through
the house like Dracula
she raped us, drew blood
satin red and smooth
She was a volcano
and lava ran unstinted
over furnishings and beds
and carpets squirmed and floundered
as if the Lough Ness monster
lurked beneath them.

She scoured the buildings,
the barn, the cowshed,
she ravished the grass
between the cobbles in the yard
like she was shaving an old man's
chin for the sacrament.

I hid. I hid in the grease
of the chestnut tree. I hid
in the elbow of the laurel
I hid in the maw of the bran
barrel. I put on my lemon dress
and lay in a field of buttercups
and Frances came.

I gathered strength
and turned my art to the darkened well
over the hill of Confey
I scooped and scraped off the viscous scum
where all life teemed in miniature
I built a temple under the lichened stone
like a father's purse where all wealth
teems in miniature
and Frances came.

Mother said it would be all right
when Frances settled down

Although she cooked like
a German General, attacked
the bright red lumps of meat
as if they were Jews, Mother said
it would be all right
when Frances settled down

I cradled my terror
hid my obstinacy
and Mother screamed: Lunacy
Frances is a jewel

I had to agree at night
when God came down and kicked
the chamber pot at the foot of my bed
I had to kneel and pray
for yeast that would rise my soul
like Christmas cake
but my soul went off like kettle steam
I tried to call it back
It was Aladdin: New souls for old
and Frances came

It's the fever, she said
as she sat like dough
on the foot of my bed
You see, mother said
it's all right now.
When the fever went I could rise
from bed, provided I dressed up warm
and avoided draughts.

I tramped the house
like a tiddly-wink I jumped
from squares into pots
I was my best toy dog
and straw came out of my chest
I was Minnie Mouse in Mother's
high-heeled shoes
But Frances owned my soul

"In safe keeping," she said
and her iceberg head
jerked widely and wisdom
snorted through her nose

Now I must pray to Frances
go on my knees at night
because Frances held my soul
between her fists like a rubber ball

But one day
one duck-egg-coloured day
Frances leaned out of the window
she leaned out and spoke
to the air like a racial memory

I stood in all this speaking
silent behind Frances
I basked in this and I was
secret as a wasp crawling into the jam

Frances was now lady-God
lady-God resting, and I was
lady-God's toy into which
she could replace my soul
like a key into a walking doll

But I was unwound and rubber
If she turned round and put her hand
on my stomach I'd say "Ma ma".

But I knew there was more to God
than just Frances. There must be proof
right inside Frances. So I crept nearer
I was moonsilence, I was Rumpelstiltskin
hiding my name
and I was unguessable, I lifted
up Frances' skirt
and flung it over her head.

You will soon be a big girl,
Mother said, and there are things
you'll learn about then.
I won't beat you limp
like a rabbit-skin but what a pity
now that everything was so ship shape
that Frances had to leave.

I swallowed my soul
and it went down like a raw potato
when Mother had seen to this
she told me that there was a girl
in the village called Myra.
Pity she's an R.C., Mother said
but it would be all right
when Myra came.

Outside the Odeon Camden Town

The snow on the street like stewed apple
the buses slopslopping past
with carton-loads of paddies.
In the illuminated cheek-bones of the Odeon
cinema
on my twentyninth birthday I waited.

An aeroplane took off in Arizona
and Buddy Holly died.

Last week, Elvis Presley
felt his chest grip the skin—felt
his shrivelled parts like an empty money belt
quiver for the last time.

I am not weeping for an old star's death
or a man stumbling in secrecy
to an appointment with a mediocre end
but myself gone forty nine with memories
of my first record-player and a bunch
of "forty-fives" and a Greek boy
separating air from vowels

"Will you come... ba...by... will you come?"

Before Going up

Before going up
she downed a pint of cooking sherry

How was it, she asked afterwards.

Good, he said, for you?

Fine.

First

A dog should die outside, the others said
but I had taken her
scrunched up in my arms,
hidden her in the shed.

We lay together in a shroud of hay
holding death aside
like the curtain in a theatre.
But then it came: the blood.
It spurted from her mouth,
spurted on the flagstones
like a string of beads.

What follows obliterates,
with each new loss,
that accident of grief.
But how can one forget what was one's
first. First anything, first love,
first loss, first kiss.

Crybaby

for John McLachlan

Her neighbours talked
with wasps in their teeth:
We heard your baby crying,
crying half the night.

Sweet chain of love, she shouted
that binds me to my child.

(She was at a party down the road
the night the host hanged himself.)

Snow Love

Dublin is not accustomed
to this thick white coat
It has crept back into silence
in a cemetery of time

With the crack of the clock
the traffic starts; slow splashing
wheels make newly furrowed lines
filthy beneath this creaking skin
while day hangs up the sun
like a plug of orange tobacco.

We are happy to be ritually forgotten
lucky to belong to this great
redundant mass on this cold day.
To be free to count each other's bones
beneath the bedclothes.

That wheeling spectacle beyond the glass
has all our sympathy, by God!
But we are free to make—repeat—
a blessing of each bone

Till the short day melts
like a candle in its saucer
and snow peters down once more
like silent falling stars.

How My True Love and I Lay Without Touching

How my true love and I lay without touching
How my hand journeyed to the drumlin of his hip
my pelvis aching
just like two saints or priests or nuns
my true love and I lay without touching.

How I would long for the brush of a kiss
to travel my cheek or the cheek of my groin
my heart aching
But just like two saints or priests or nuns
my true love and I lay without touching.

Last night in my dreams I spoke with his wife
his true love who had left him surely as they lay without
touching
my heart for her was aching
For like two saints or priests or nuns
the two loves once lay without touching

But the dream of her faded before concentrating
each to each in our innocent mutual hating
her hand aching
to blind me with bullets to prevent herself from pining
for a once love she longed for and lay without touching.

Now my true love lies in the mutton of madness
"I was always troubled by sex," he says, with great sadness
his wife and I aching
in our cold single beds with many seas dividing
as we think of the years we spent without touching.

From a Painting by Artemisia Gentileschi

How strange to be wielding this knife
with such violence
Regard the bounce of muscle on my arms
between my fingers the scarlet beads
of victory.

Who is beneath my bloodied hand
(If they name me wanton then I am
as is he between my nimble fingers)
But for convenience I have named him Holofernes
and she? The woman hacking off his head?
I call her Judith (how pretty in comparison
her handmaid—assistant in this direful deed
Great gentle hands—the midwife
hovering over the labour bed.)

I do not pierce my breast with thorns
the red rose has no song for me.
(Rose—white my bosom—pure—
clean as foam on the crest of a wave.
I cleanse my palette with this violent act.)
Later I shall paint the humble, the heroic.

Chain Strokes

The breathing began at eight p.m.
Two starched nurses—angry swans—
In my head the sonata—B flat minor—
That was my sleep
Restless chromatic quavers.

I awoke
Lento. Again lento.

She died at eight a.m.

Ten years later
I read *Sons and Lovers*.

Exiles

for Geraldine O'Reilly

Those were the seedlings we sowed
pricked and primed against the hard
rock of poverty.

Those were the seedlings—
We have put names on their
children. The children
of Gurley Flynn and Mother Jones—
Oh your america.

Tumbletown and Dead River Valley
famine-forced they crowded the canals
from the bog of Allen to Idaho,
crossed the Atlantic
in the stench of homelessness.

Now Bridie don't forget to say your prayers

Mother get me a bride
from out the four green fields—
my fields.

Mean fields.

Some hid behind the lace
others shed stone tears
Useless tears

To hell with the bleeding fingers
of all the women
(a nickel a day, make hay make hay)
cooking fat at night
in the quiver of the candle

We'll show you who the boss is
you Irish bitches.

Now Bridie keep your legs crossed
and the rosary between your toes

But they rose . . . rose . . .
like bonfires on a mountain
every mansheila of them
rose against the whips
broke files, made unions.
It was a slow going
a slow coming.

Dear Bridie I received the dollars.
your father's taken ill
I got shoes for Peadar
and Kathleen
I'll put the rest by
Pray for me

Why are we waiting?
Give me the D.C. 9
New York, New World
New suitcase, transit visa

Dear Uncle Tom get me a husband
and a Green Card
And I'll never leave
your america

My Green Card

Mean Card.

This is your pilot
Pointing Pilot
Feathering down on Kennedy Airport

Oh America!

I strike out now
in a skyscrape of desire
shivering for dollars
You mean I've come all the way from Clontarf
And there's no job?

Why is everyone sleeping
in the subway?

These are the seedlings we sow
pricked and primed against
the hard rock of poverty

We put names on these children
the children of Gurlay Flynn
and Mother Jones

Oh your america.

Remembering the Blindness of Jorge Luis Borges

He went off last year
to—I hope—some far-seeing place
At that fearsome Taoiseach do
I took his quilted hand
barely murmuring how honoured
I was to meet him
With Byronic irony he muttered
So is everyone else.

De donde viene este vino?
In that dark world
we were invisible accomplices
bandits without a cause
banderillos without a bull.

Penumbra—shadow—poet of eternal light.

Breach Baby

Black panther he does not
streak through forests.
Back and forth, back and forth
in this house of his.
In this house of his, he paces.

My son who is gone five—
the solitary watcher—
says quietly:

"He does not know which way."

He remembers my rib-cage.

Pointless

You go on and on.

But imagine the world without music.
Just imagine—no fifths, no thirds,
no arpeggios, no atonal notes.
(And surely God invented the octave.)

I once saw a horse dance in Phoenix Park.

Yes you go on and on
saying art, unless political, is pointless
But you don't pick blackberries with me
you are not interested in mud.

Clondalkin Concrete

Late again! You know we keep regular hours
in Clondalkin Concrete.

I was the Temp.
The one who worked from five past nine till six
with no let up
But they kept regular hours at Clondalkin Concrete

From Clondalkin Concrete I wrote a letter to Paul
I told him I was writing concrete verse
and very soon I would send them, block on clock
in Clondalkin Concrete we keep stanzas
numbered and counted carefully, cement and sand.
We keep regular poems in Clondalkin Concrete

All the while I worked in Clondalkin Concrete
I must have sold a million tons of blocks
I was a bungalow blitz of a typist
Invoice neat in my work
But I wrote, Dear Paul, I dedicate to you
every block of a concrete stanza
every freezing grain of sand
For I'm up to my neck in Clondalkin Concrete

While directly gazing into my boss's watery studs
All that Fall, I shouted, All that Fall

Moth Dust

Pumpkin fond pumpkin
had water under the chin
It didn't matter.
It didn't matter then, until
his eyes became two asterisks
his back a scythe
and with his dainty fingers
he filled my mouth with sloes
my mind with moth dust.

But he left Mahomed's thumbprint
on my shoulder.

Her Sister's Child

Her sister's child is sleeping with her husband
and she is not a bit surprised.
He loved her far too much to stake his all,
(he said); she's not so sure,
the baby leaves his bed at five.

Her sister's child is blonde and bonnie and blithe,
at twenty-one a little immature
(perhaps a little indiscreet?)
should be more circumspect, you'd think.

When she is far away
and still alive she'll tell
this story with more subtlety.

After Pushkin

A pinch of laughter opened up his face
"Irish?" he said. "Ireland!"
"What do you do there really?"
With O a wave of nonchalance, "You know," I said
"Write poems, books, you know, that sort of thing—
waste a lot of trees . . ."

A ring of comprehension, "Rabbie Burns" he said.
"Ah no, that other lot—O'Casey, Joyce—
different kettle of Celtic fish"

"I see," he said, his tiny specs
transparent flowers of recognition
"The Portrait, him I know, I like him much—
I just stamp passports."

I had stepped across his threshold
from this pin in the Atlantic
and placed my brief amongst the idols
and the pictures—Akhmatova, Osip and Nadezhda—
The Rubens, Caravaggios, Matisses—
All histories combine—and he
who takes no part in this idiot
warp and woof of words
gazes at me sternly from his window,
nodding, sees how turning in a circle
everything comes round.

Memory

I remember my mother who hated onions
sex and mongrel dogs,
my father's rusty fingers
wading through butterflies.
So I grew to talk kindly with enemies,
soldiers and policemen.
I stare into the morphine of memory
pressing the needle into the weakest spot.

I wonder does she hold her skirt around her knees
in the heaven she believed in,
the demon sex beaten to a dish-cloth
with semi-colons of thou shalt nots
full stops of self abasement
or does she lie, legs splayed out
for dogs and pictures and others to enter her
face glazed in anticipation
for something she never experienced before.

Last week I visited her grave
a dead wreath had landed askew the weathered cross.
Good day, Ma, I said and lifted the crumbling crown
and hurled it into the fields of Confey.

On Mistaking a Jesuit Lecture for a Poetry Reading

Is this the poetry reading?
Shh… all heads turn in my direction.
I settle down beside a balding man
and listen to the speaker.
He tells of Paris, nineteen eighty eight
of how the doors are open every day
I wait to hear how poets have been entertained
and housed and watered freely
but not a word of verse or stanza
crutch or limp is coming from his lips.
This is a long long intro, think I
looking at the man whose rim of hair
is tonsure like
(but surely tonsures have gone out, think I)
he sneers unfriendlily, I draw my breath
uncross my knees, look round for the three poets
I came to hear. No poet. No familiar face
and then the awful truth!
I am the only woman in the place.
Ahem, I mutter through my tonsils
Where do you think I am?
A howl of shhishes echoes from the ashtray walls
Mr Tonsure very nearly spits.
Now my buttocks are experiencing the sting
of tensing muscles—my knee has gone to sleep
I dare not move. I feel like shouting "Fire"
or anything that might get me out
but everything's against me, doors are closed
no doubt I am locked in. Perhaps I'm dead
and this is where the wretched sinners
go—to poetry readings in the sky
where smoking is forbidden
and Jesuits interminably drool
about the good that they have done below
and no poet sings.

Lion

Grandpa paced the avenue,
Tired old lion—
Forwards, turn and back
as though with every step
his luggage lightened
as though the years
were falling back
to the hide-and-seek
of childhood

He said he'd die on Wednesday
On Tuesday, a wintry night,
clouds buffeting, no moon,
he took his final walk.
He stopped just once
to pat his pockets
to reassure himself
he'd jettisoned the dross,
shook out his chalk-white mane
and climbed the stairs.

At the funeral my grandma said
"He was a meticulous gentleman."

Dostoevsky's Grave

I am locked in this acropolis
just Feodor and me
I rub my fingers
in his overcoat of stone
gambling my airline ticket
and find in the valley
of my life-line
the gravel of Baden Baden

In Memoriam John Jordan

We were long on the one bitch road
between the "Hatch" and that "Low" Leeson Street
Haring through Agatha Christies (you)
or on some parched afternoon
we'd bump into a waiting moment
with a how d'you do how are you
(as Eddie Maguire used to say)
Or your apocryphal pronouncement
"May God forgive me, all my enemies
down at one go."

In Grogan's bar with mongering dole-men
adroop or clattering drunk
The silent country of your endurance
was something that stepped aside
however insecure the footing
uninviting the ravines
Conversing with that other John
a Chaplinesque half sided smile
an Oh dear me, to save a fall or two.

After the fireworks have subsided
we will sing old songs
La recherche du temps perdu
and birds will call as though incensed.

Dawn Guest

My patch of lawn between poplar and oak
is empty once again. For a moment
in an agony of pride he raised his antlers
whipped the wind, leapt and was gone.

Perhaps he was never there
between oak and poplar
this dawn visitor. Too much beauty
destroys the levels of concentration

But ever since I've watched this patch of grass
as if he still was there—sinews locked for flight
as though we could in one split second
give skin for skin, muscle for rippling muscle.

Still he lives on in my mind's eye
What I've invested in him
like an episode of tremendous luck
The pot of gold at the end of the rainbow.

Brother

If only he would admit to being born
my brother. Every Christmas, without fail,
a cheque arrives—the nervous cutting of the knife—
it goes up yearly with inflation.
Hastily I post my New Year Card—the feast is over—
clip off another piece of guilt
like breaking off an edge of biscuit.

I know that he'll outlive me
this wombless man. He'll pay
the undertaker, scowl mysteriously
at my friends—a motley crew—
later he'll read my obituary in the press
and find out things he never knew.

History Stopped that Night

It might have been anyone
but the fact that it was I
who lay in a mulch of leaves
between two ice-ages
watching your face in shadow
speckled like seed-cakes
in a bronze moon-madness, harvest for size
made me wonder at luck that
makes a twist of time so unimportant. Morning. I woke
a shelf of moss had curled itself into a pillow
it was damp and cold. And you slept deep I think

History had undone itself like buttons on a coat
We had played farms and families for centuries
of weeping land—gone off—made good or bad
adopted transatlantic ways and accents
become colonial, racist, over-sentimental
the hovel of our past made glorious
in the quick buck game, and fuck the wogs.

My duty then was to make sure
that he who lay beside me woke that day
though mulch and hypnum might invade
our nostrils all too soon
beneath the forest-floor of someone else's sorrow.

But coming from the hostelry that night
we'd kissed each other flat
and mottled by moon light
fallen like Icarus in history's flight.

Letter to My Teacher

I am speeding the Esker townland
on my fairy cycle.
I am seven and the day is grained
with a fine Kildare mist.
It is moist as a bull's nose.
I drive my face into it as into a wash-tub,
my neck cools. At the edge of the golf-course
a lorry passes; mud cakes like chocolate
on my socks.

They have thrown me out for writing poems.
Now I am telling you this before I die
I am telling you this in a letter.
Poems were bad they said
so from seven on I knew.
Iris Wellwood you were my teacher,
Iris Wellwood of the sun-red hair,
come all the way from Cavan town
to throw me out for writing poems.

Now I've been thrown out from everywhere
pubs, houses, public transport
and the only reason far's I know
is that frogs keep jumping off the paper
mosquitoes dancing in the cubic yard
of my skull from Leeson Street to Kopovar
from Leningrad on the Nevsky Prospekt
to Clanbrassil Street on the *Villamos*.

You taught me seven nines were sixty-three
but writing poems was a waste of time
I write this letter with sincerest thanks
now that nine times seven years
are nearly gone. I've ridden that fairy bike
a long long way from Esker, Confey or Spion Kop
through the earliest townlands of my mind
the townlands of *Muslin* and *Esther Waters*.

Note

for Jacqueline Bardwell

The trouble is I miss the short sea
in an alcove of rock or the wider
more impelling stretch of the Atlantic
I seem to be paralysed between two Drumlins
and the trees against the pewter clouds
unnerve me as though to say "I know your number".

Still at the moment, all is well
and when the time is right
I shall go—there are other places
somewhere with a Russian wind talking down the chimney
and the Black Sea breaking wilfully
beyond the reaches of Chekhov's garden.

C.T. Scan

They've put my head inside the big machine.
Jack the cat stalks round my brain.
He purrs, he kneads,
his paws are soft as mushrooms.
He has triumphant eyes.

They talk casually
on the intercom
about stomach pills and airline sickness.

I lie still as stone in this aluminium trunk
thinking of Mary Shelley

A Single Rose

I have willed my body to the furthering of science.
Although I'll not be there
to chronicle my findings
I can imagine all the students
poring over me:
"My God, is that a liver?
And those brown cauliflowers are lungs?"
"Yes, sir, a fine example of how not to live."
"And what about the brain?"
"Alas the brain. I doubt if this poor sample
ever had one." As with his forceps
he extracts a single rose.

Roses

My aunt Joyce had the roses
roses of consumption
two round rose buds
blood red roses
roses of consumption
on her cheeks.

In the teeming Mayo rain
every year in the hired house
was when we heard the sea say "Joyce".
We children heard it—"Joyce"—
while the waves dragged back the stones
with a terrifying "oh".

We'd offer her the silence of the mirror
a powder puff, a comb,
and bundled in all kinds of coats
we'd carry her to Ballycastle, Glenamoy, Belderg or Bunnahowen,
anywhere the sea would growl her name
and she could sit and listen quietly.

But they were cleverer than we
with pills and pillows; in the end a wooden box
they laid her in it like you would a bunch of flowers
in a shoe box—roses maybe
and then we heard the thump of roses
earth and roses—roses
like the blood red roses on her cheeks

The Price of Shoes in Russia

I am an old old woman, *Izvinite*
My fingers are nicotine brown
from endless fags. But I exult
in the wings of the choir
that swing from within
the walls of the cathedral.

Till another old old woman,
older even than I, jumps on me
with the speed of hate
cleaves my head with her umbrella
and calls her grandson to evict me.

Being no fool in my eightieth year
I stuff the burning orb into my pocket
Izvinite I am old and stupid as a dog
I beg forgiveness on my hands and knees.
He tells me his name is Yuri.

Yes I'm Yuri—Yuri from Kharkov
And I'm an ancient Protestant woman
from a Catholic country called Ireland
and I wish I'd never smoked
in the precincts of his church.
Oh Yuri, I cry. But Yuri does not beat me.
He sits me down in the mellow shadow of a tree
near the puddled fish pond in the park
and talks of shoes.

Shoes, he says, lighting up,
are very dear in Kharkov.
I take his Cosmos gratefully, inhale and cry
Oh yes, but they are also dear in Dublin
Shoes in Dublin are exceptionally dear.

But socks, he cries, we queue for socks
Not to mention stockings I say.
He is shaken with a fine delight
as we work our way up thighwards

and I burn slowly—from inside with a scorching love
from my pocket from the burning cigarette
and from the sun above my double vented skull.

When we embrace we agree to meet in Yalta
and feed cyclamen seeds through the eyelids
of Chekhov's dacha.

The Bingo Bus

In Killinarden there was nothing—
Nothing—but nearer town
there was the Bingo Bus

The Bingo Bus, the Bingo Bus
Nearer to Thee, my God, the Bingo Bus
And Strip the Willow, they played
With the driver, trussed the conductor—
Danced Turkey in the Straw.

Every Thursday without fail
The ladies rode on the Bingo Bus

And Booze before Bingo and after
And lots of Booze in between
Returning late from Bingo
They ate the conductor whole.

We in Killinarden, wanted, O so much
To have a Bingo Bus of our own

We wrote to the Authorities,
Begged and begged on our knees
T.D.s were hammered, we marched,
Made flags, went on hunger strike
Outside the Dáil.

You lot aren't ready for Bingo,
You've only been here a year,
You must have lots more babies
Before you deserve a Bingo Bus.

So every year to the clinic
Three out, one in, four out, one in
But still no Bingo Bus

I had to leave Killinarden
Wearied from making flags,
Marching and lobbying and having kids
So I moved right into a hotel.
St. Brendan's is its name

I make sanitary towels for bingo players
I do my bit for bingo players
I am on the ball for bingo players
I'm saving up for bingo
Saving up for bingo

Lila's Potatoes

They asked me to write a poem
about Lila's potatoes
I thought about the eighteen forties
I thought about watercress
I thought about weeds
but they were black
my plants were black
lazy beds, they said, were O.K

I had spent my life in lazy beds
one way and another—lazy beds
in and out of lazy beds

They'd got me everywhere
when I slept in different towns,
places, seas,—another child
lazy beds, they said, were OK in the famine

I saw my plants—black—leaves black
stalks black—lazy beds, they said—
in the famine—lazy beds

So I made kids in lazy beds—strapping women
all all from lazy beds—eight altogether
they got jobs in underground London pubs,
strip halls—make-believe—run around
and ended up in lazy beds all eight of them

Lazy beds make black potatoes—Lila's potatoes
have the blight—lazy beds—Lila's potatoes
they got the blight

Then Seamus took the bad luck out of it
It was the sun, he said, caused it.
I often wondered what caused all my children.
I'm glad it was the sun.

Thems Your Mammy's Pills

for Edward McLachlan

They'd scraped the top soil off the garden
and every step or two they'd hurled a concrete block
bolsters of mud like hippos from the hills
rolled on the planters plantings of the riff-raff of the city.

The schizophrenic planners had finished off their job
folded their papers, put away their pens—
the city clearances were well ahead.

And all day long a single child was crying
while his father shouted: Don't touch them,
thems your mammy's pills.

I set to work with zeal to play 'Doll's House',
'Doll's Life', 'Doll's Garden'
while my adolescent sons played 'Temporary Heat'
in the living room out front
and drowned the opera of admonitions:
Don't touch them, thems your mammy's pills.

Fragile as needles the women wander forth
laddered with kids, the unborn one ahead
to forge the mile through mud and rut
where mulish earth-removers rest, a crazy sculpture.

They are going back to the city for the day
this is all they live for—
going back to the city for the day.

The line of shops and solitary pub
are camouflaged like check points on the border
the supermarket stretches emptily
a circus of sausages and time
the till-girl gossips in the veg department
Once in a while a woman might come in
to put another pound on
the electronic toy for Christmas.

From behind the curtains every night
the video lights are flickering, butcher blue
Don't touch them, thems your mammy's pills.

No one has a job in Killinarden
nowadays they say it is a no-go area
I wonder, then, who goes and does not go
in this strange forgotten world
of video and valium.

I visited my one time neighbour
not so long ago. She was sitting
in the hangover position.
I knew she didn't want to see me
although she'd cried when we were leaving.

I went my way
through the quietly rusting motor cars and prams,
past the barricades of wire, the harmony of junk.
The babies that I knew are punk-size now
and soon children will have children
and new voices ring the leitmotif:

Don't touch them, thems your mammy's pills.

An Unusual Irish Summer

for Nicholas McLachlan

I ask them have they brought the galleys
I am alive and awake with a hole in my head.
My son's face swings above me
like an extraordinary coin
I'd been dreaming of water chestnuts
and the heat beneath my skull
makes me long for that apron of sand
stretching out to the country's eye
in an unusual Irish summer.

Kassia

Kassia, the 9th century Byzantine poet
wore epigrams like bangles on her arms
when offered marriage with the emperor
she scalded him with wit.

Banished from the court
Columns of stone will kneel
she said, before you change a fool.

A learned fool, God save us.
The pigs are eating pearls.

Skipping Banville in Barcelona

for Colm Tóibín

I am infinitely caused
beneath the pinnacles of Gaudi
Mesmerising struts, angels,
apostles, dog-lion
timber and stone
"There are no straight lines
in nature" Gaudi said.

The quilted edifice towers
twin pinnacles (God can only
see downwards) religious
phalluses—bourgeois trinkets
gingerbread and wine

Retiring afterwards to remember
and cool down I pick up the Book of Evidence
watch Carmen being murdered once again
remember previous jealousies and loves
and spend the evening
skipping Banville in Barcelona.

Maggie's Cottage

for Geraldine Whelan

There we kept time pressed apart
like a row of books supported by two book-ends
there we erased the pitch and toss
of all the lives we'd lived—
the pot holes of disaster.

The "where oh where" of now is the question of that time
when as Vladimir and Estragon we walked the avenue
with our water bottles of laughter, our occasional fights
We flew saucers of friendship above the stars
which landed in the lap of the "big house"
as when dawn brought the demon Harding to cook our
breakfast complete with pike and hangover.

If the snake of time has shed its skin again
I know that artichokes are different from thistles.
We left our marks—a painted room—a broken pane of glass
a hedge of beans, a colony of spinach.

Poems in Periodicals
& from Bardwell's Papers

2000s

The Colour Orange

for Brian Keenan

The man with the skin
The man within
The man in the bright light, silent
The Atlantic beyond the window
The face behind the window
The face at an angle
The man remembers the colour orange
The colour of the orange
The ribbed texture
Of the orange skin
The man within the skin
The skin's the man's cage
The Atlantic beyond
The memory of no light
And no colour orange.

Birth

In this solitary room
nothing moves until
a bee falls with a thump
on the lino. It is then
that the wind bends
the window and the world
switches its axis
and your voice echoes
echoes in my bloodstream:
they are letting me out
and I have nowhere to go.

And Every Crocus Laid

Strange how nature never learns
Throws everything up
hastily, ignoring time
and then is surprised when the storm
subsides and all its tricks
and jokes fall flat.
Yes, this March, like any other,
is sprinkled with poor dead heads
Tiny purple tear drops saying
at least we tried.

Life Behind

Why are old women so skinflinty?
Snarl and whimper or take to alcohol
their erstwhile laurels thrown aside
like last year's Christmas ivy
or left dusty on the picture frame
gathering motes of memories
family reunions

Is it because there is no silk left
of flesh or hands to run smooth
as the zephyr across a longing bone
It is because, in the case of marriage
they sleep in separate rooms
meet unlovely at breakfast, scored
by silence, a radio blaring.
Songs whispering romance
as though love was simple

Who knows the ache in the old woman's
groin, the eyes have to turn in
away from what others see
the mouth perpetually smiling
the death so near a welcome
and a fear. Who knows what
longing means when there is no hope

Sure the life behind was good
That's what the others say.
But mostly bad; you grew your
children badly, extorted their
wealth, their dress of knowing
their future always ahead
your present every step into the past
The last moment when each one
left the nest and you said "Ah
a spot of freedom at last." For what?
For no man—why you can't imagine—
wants a woman who aches for improbables.
And cannot see the lines that grit
her hands and face.

from

The White Beach

(Salmon Poetry, 1998)

*

nineties

Matisse Woman

The woman emerges
two-dimensional.
She presses into the wall,
slides off her clothes,
removing the cover
of the transfer.
But the sudden hues remain—
polka dots—the splash
of blood on the vase—
peonies, violets
sprayed against the curtain.
She smiles, her body opens
to produce a child.
Where has he gone? they ask.
She points to the belly

but there is no birth
only the shadows of leaves
tracing the twilight
of her skin.

She Tried To Be a Woman Twice

She tried to be a woman
brought him the oranges of love,
on trays of malachite,
coddled the egg
exactly as he liked it.
She ghosted an evergiving
smile—a wraith above the bed,
bleached her mind
to match his evenly,
shivered at his touch.

Branded thus she bore him sons,
tidied away the genes,
when the last one came.
She withdrew gently as night
proves itself into day, knowing
for a brief time her dawn.

The second time she wearied to his will
her skull expanded, her heart
bled its secrets into his sieve.
Her days lay down upon each other,
her protective soul, no longer
weatherproof, let in the storm.

The empty chair, uneaten meats,
the angry shoulders
told their history—her story
wandered off—a body into sleep.

Moments

for Edward McLachlan

No moon slides over Harcourt Terrace.
The canal is black. The barracks
crouches on her left.
She sees the child. He holds his coat
across his chest. On his hands,
old socks blunt his fingers.
The handle of his fishing net
has snapped.

Sleep escapes the old woman
on her angry couch. Such images
assault, torment and tease
the sense of her.
Time rolls back on its silent wheels,
empties itself into moments.

How many guilts can one human endure.
One human in all the world, alone
one man or woman holding moments
of a child running, holding shut his coat
with socks on his hands.

Song of the African Boy

Oh Sligo, my Africa,
I am black
and my mother
brings home the shopping
in two Quinnsworth bags.

Oh Sligo, my Africa,
I own a donkey
and a pair of runners,
did I tell you I was black
and my mother does the shopping?

Oh Sligo, my Africa,
I knew you my father
from darkest Islington
for as long as it took
to drop your semen
into my mother's womb.

And I shall grow tall and black
in Sligo, my Africa
and the bowline will slip
from the harbour
to the blunting of the sea.

I will let my mother
walk those long miles
from Quinnsworth
while I shrug my shoulders
at the feet
of the continent's shelf.

Oh Sligo, my Africa,
break the long silence
that is my quarter.

My mother doesn't chide me
because the palms of my hands
are pink
but I know how she feels
on the long road
when the yellow iris nods.

He Begs Her to Stay

Please stay, the chevaux de frise
won't last forever.

She can't listen. She thinks
I can't lie here day after day
while the mind fingers
the barriers.

We must enter together
the boutique of loneliness
and fill our baskets.

Two Lessons in Anatomy: York Street, Dublin

LESSON I *(i.m. The X Case)*

The father of the pregnant girl
has lost his temper—their bodies
reflected in the armour of rush hour traffic.
Two people from one kitchen.

She rubs her eyes like a cat
polishing its face with a single paw.
His anger spins from the bones of his shoulders
with the crescendo of his curses.

She backs away, knocking into students,
bruising her ankle on the pedal of a bike.
She will go to that nowhere place
where decisions bang around in her head.
I wonder will she remember the time
the moth was banging against the electric bulb
and how she climbed on that wobbly chair
to cup the insect in her palm
to throw it from the open window.

LESSON II

The woman upstairs is being beaten.
Her screams jangle across the street
where windows in the College of Surgeons
black out one by one. Students
are filtering home to their digs
in Rathmines or Ranelagh
and the air is left untroubled
by the cry for help
that no lessons in anatomy can fathom.

Dancing with Beezy in Jordan's Pub

With country and western suit
gangster tie, bell bottoms
he sings to us

Dancing with Beezy in Jordan's

As gangster guest
in this company
the soft shoe rhythm
tidies away the throb:

Will you waltz, my love,
Will you waltz with me
again

We women talk of rain
and chemotherapy.

Three Ages to Midnight

She took the cross-bar
all the way to Kilcock
on the midnight hour
of Plough Monday
conceived a son
carried him back
by the light
of the Milky Way
born nine moons after
on the hill of Annamult.

At the periphery of Clare
they bundled into a dance-hall
Are ye from Mars, married, single,
lost? No she's married to midnight
on the Prairie by Ennistymon
and lives with Sean
the cowgirl's man.

She is the oldest witch in Cloughboley
grandmother to midnight
callgirl to the moon.
She eats hare's feet and atropine
manages badly on her income
of Bulls Blood and Kerosene.

Ghost Story

Beyond the horse-hair rain
on the windscreen,
the hare jumps—
a fleeting nod from the rhododendrons.

There's only a headlight glint
between driver and corpse—
so perfect, so other-worldly,
you can't blame the rain for everything.

Next night the driver went that road,
the rain-man flagged him down
in his old torn mac, he thumbed a lift
and they drove together silently.

The driver saw the dark brown fur
on the rain-man's wrist,
watched the man's ears growing,
the nose twitching.
Please don't do this to me,
the driver said.

Aha, said the man in the long torn coat
arched his beautiful back and sniffed the air.
You can drop me by the rhododendrons,
You can't blame the rain for everything.

Blow In

She came
with her pile of books
her manuscripts
her published works.

She took her stance
the men parenthesised their pints
to stare. Some welcomed,
others shifted. Restless
crafts in their harbour.

So brash in her folly
she thought to take
the heavy sea and storm
it into her breast. To lift
the slap, the suck.

Did she not come
to learn the ABC
the classroom sums
how two and two don't always
make the tidy count.

No one moved until
she tried to prove
she was the college girl
she'd learn and poise her pen
but listless in this knowledge
they split her like a log.

Yet for quite some time
they took her in.
Bowing to the tradition
of hospitality—
guests are welcome for a time—
when you've drunk their wine
you ought to leave
with dignity. Take with you
the coat they've offered you
and wear it right.

Playing Tennis with Eamonn

If, as is the view, tennis is sinful
I sinned on the back line
for twenty double faults.
O Lord forgive me for sinning on the back line
of the asphalt tennis court
in Tuosist, County Kerry.

Eamonn, a stocky lad of some ten years
beat me six love, six love
And I in my eightieth year
not all that nimble on my pins
took love easy on the back line
on the back line of the tennis court
in Tuosist, County Kerry.

But in the third set, oh the third set
with my splintering back hand
I had him on the gallop.
Haring from one side of the court
to the other, Eamonn, ten year old Eamonn
was hard put with his returns.
And my lobs—you've never seen lobs like them
they soared like gulls in the pouring rain
far above the tennis court, the asphalt tennis court
in Tuosist, County Kerry.

And after my twentieth double fault
my serves skimmed into the right hand corner
creating pebbles of asphalt to scatter in the flood,
globules of asphalt, craters of asphalt
bullets of asphalt as the water logged ball

slithered and Eamonn, gibbering with ten year old rage
played fast and loose with forbidden curses
cursing rain, me, asphalt and Tuosist.

I picked up my crutches and tottered home
to the cornerstone of the Kingdom,
the soaking corner of the Beara Peninsula,
the wettest corner of Western Europe.

Eamonn pissed off to his dinner.

Cynic on the Rock

for Dermot Seymour

I watch him watching the sea
I've come from a city
of glass domes, streets
dancing with useless sentences
I want to tell him
out there the mind jumps and scatters
a townscape of no walls.

He bows to the crescendo of the gale
the sea shakes out its petticoats.

What can I say to him?
That I am trying to buy time
create a shell in this white horizon
to find in this enormity of sea and sky
a jot, a new word at the very end
of the dictionary.

Tell me, he says, without turning,

Is there wind in Belfast?

My Old Aberdeen

The heel of a shoe
taps three four three four.
Someone dances
in someone else's head.

A voice cries:
Come on Mary, sing
Give her a hand, everyone.

In a cathedral of silence
she sings:

My Old Aberdeen
and no one wants to know.

An old man with a curious limp says:
it would make a dog think.

Nothing Else

for Nicholas McLachlan

Cloonagh, below the sweep
of Ardtrasna, a pocket unfilled
where the hill rises. Trá Bhán
the beach where the barge buckled
in '95 and bothered us
with possibilities. Trá Bhán
no longer white but sheeted over
with shloch and crannach and rock
limestone steps to the blow-hole
under the alt, is the end of the road
and nothing else.

Above this crescent
I share my house with time
and nothing else
gaze at the pictures of my children
who have treated me well
for my imagination
but pass me by as the wind passes the house
and takes its sigh with it.

Dog Ear

I am turning my death over
like a page in a book
I dog-ear it.
I need to remember the place.

Post Card

I drift to sleep,
thinking of the blow-hole under the alt
and wondering about a sea lion
I once met.

I dream then of the window
and fingers walking.
A post card is pushed
under the door.
It comes in with the rain
which obliterates the message.

January 1st '95, the Party's Over

The party ended yesterday.
Pocket whiskey gone the roads,
fundamentals packed.

The sea in party frock
punched the air, slapped in '95.
The mountain moved across the light.

The cat crossed the moon at 2 a.m.
shirking the secret of dawn.
The mind won't clear that easy.

The party ended yesterday
pocket whiskey gone the roads,
the new light leaves you unprepared.

The Dead Child's Arm Washed up on the Beach

The dog brought
the arm of the child
ulna to radius

fingers wrested
from the ocean's pillow.

The dog took the bones
to the other child.

He who lives
thinking of that other he
the child

who picked up the bones
with the dead hand
reaching ulna

crossing the radius
to the wrist
of that other child.

White the bones
of the children, white
the lace of the sea's kiss.

Hale-Bopp

i.m. Martin Healy , d. 5th March 1997

I'll sit one more day
in the chair, or even
walk out to test the night
to hover in the wet grass,
trying to catch sight
of a comet.

Cuckoo on top of the Protestant Church, Dugort

Cuckoo, Cuckoo, Cuculus Canorus,
remarkable bird. I heard you
yesterday winging your way
to drop your bastard egg
in someone else's house.

Who's afraid of your cuckoo-spit
your lady's smock your
ragged robin dress?

Cuckoo, Cuckoo, Cuculus Canorus,
from bed to bed hop skip
and jump. Frog-hopper
Protestant church-goer
over the trees and up.

Cuckoo, Cuckoo, yes
I heard you yesterday
here there and everywhere
summer-harbinger, bad bird,
liar, egg-dropper.

I like your nerve,
Cuculus Canorus,
gate crasher
percher on steeples.
Such selfishness,
such panache
never in the one place
twice.

No Return

They tried to recapture
the days of Leonard Cohen.
Dylan, the Beatles
as they downed a bottle of Bush,
sang unmusically, fell
into the bed.

It was a belated effort—
two desperadoes on a sinking ship
no pirate of passion
to storm the bulwark.
They laughed at last,
remembering the mornings
of Black Russian cigarettes.

Mad Mrs Sweeney

For one whole year
I've watched Mad Sweeney
above in his branch.

He has forgotten how to fly
and stares down at me.
Occasionally he spits.

Today I plucked up courage
to address him.

Mad Sweeney, I said,
I am madly in love with you.

If you'd just bend down that wing
and give me a hike

I'd be up and away,
space shuttle to the moon.

He fluffs his plumage
in that acid way he has

strops his beak
on an outgoing twig.

Well at least shake down a feather
and I'll culture it
with a ball of seaweed

and when it has grown full size
I'll fly to the top of your tree

and be mad Mrs Sweeney
gone in the head but heart whole.

Granuaile's Tower
Kildavnet, Achill

Eyrie on the storm's rim
breakneck descent
mist mystery, heel
of the sound—one
of her many hides.
Wild woman—high perch.
They built them strong then
castles, women, walls.

Seasons

Autumn

Weeds through the curragh's ribs
Grass on the jinnet's hames
Rust on the tall ship's anchor

God's acre splits
Cow moans, tumbles
Kestrel defines the wind

Arranged in this landscape
I await the wound of winter
The coming of the geese

Spring

The moon aligns the sun
The ocean gathers

The weeds search for light
The ring of the eye expands

The scar of the torrent knits
The boulders flatten

The hares rut
The rhizomes shiver

The loam breathes
The earthworms sing

Ewe at the Corner

Every day she is at the corner
with her February twins;
a mother at the crossroads
waiting for the school bus.

Poor sheep confused
mud-black face
fleece in tangles.

Down at the harbour
they are turning over the boats
whipping the winter
out of the holds.
There's a wink of sea-strife
on the dunes.
The Northern hemisphere
races from spring to spring.

Back in the cities
mothers entangled with children
are waiting for the school bus.

Poems in Periodicals
& from Bardwell's Papers

River

The wife of the man
who lay beside the river
all his life, has allowed
his terrible thirst
to leave her at last

Her knowing, yet saying "No
I don't want the river
to change its course
It will run, always
if the want is there
I'll be the one
to stand by the rapids
where the otters play."

The Climb

The Irishman can't stop talking
The Andes fall away
in their gypsy colourings
tip sideways to the bird—
A vulture, slow, determined
as an auctioneer in the business
of marking down
the victim of the sale

The Irishman tells us: if they come
we must give them everything
clothes, money, car
Never mind the guerrillas
they are on the other side.

And finally in an elbow
of the mountains called the puna
the clouds are rolled up tight
Bouncing in the distance
like dough balls
And the machete of heat
cuts through us, sadistic
and casual as the bargain of life
in these parts is
marked down further every day,
as each man goes about his business

The Descent

On the way back the Irishman tells us
he has only one eye
as the cliff swings away below
a thousand foot drop on his blind side
and the road twists beneath us
like a jettisoned necktie
We again watch the vulture
a perfect gent, the Irishman says,
no need for burials round here
It comes quick, the end,
like falling asleep while driving.

Long Distance Bus

The man behind me snores
G'dolph…down…g'dolph…down
Across the aisle a baby fidgets
and drives his mother mad
The driver has his sleeves
rolled up, he has that casual look
all drivers have as they
unpeel the miles.
Outside the fields pass by
cows run, sheep don't
New houses rise with mobile toys
parked casually outside
what evidence of continuity
And then some unnamed hamlet
stalls the bus and one young woman
hauls the buggy, baby under arm
A man with fiery cheekbones
climbs up wearily behind her.
The bus is early
so we wait. Behind the bus stop sign
a chemist's shop displays its recognition
of the past. Tall earthen jars, glass phials,
and ads for Epsom Salts,
all a little dusty. There is silence
in this isolated village
catching the sunlight, morning clean
as though the day had forgotten to begin
The man and woman and their child
have swept away all trace of life
as though a plague was there and every one
was dead. At last the bus moves off
The driver shuffles his body
as the bus speeds up. Soon we are deep
inside a barren country. Distant sheep
are dotted on a hill like lice on a dull green
blanket. We are the whole world
in this travelling universe, It's only
the "Going" that matters.

February

February. My birth month
has brought back my pride
I can shake out my despair
where the moon rinses the tide
with silver stripes across the bay

I search through the shucks of syllables
for sense, like translating kilometres
into miles; the syntax laughs
we don't make parables that easy
With Leonard Cohen lyrics

Today I met an old man
who borrowed a ruler
to measure out his patch
the priest had left him.
There is a patch in my skull

that knits. I'll take a song
and measure mine. Grave diggers
need insurance. My children

Are my brothers and sisters
for them I purge the water
from the fishers. The curragh
rides the anarchic sea
nothing is stranger than a body
bobbing in an unexpected tide

The surface sealed
like sweat on skin
when the sheets are twisted
into frenzied bolsters

then comes the time
we can't say sorry

Workshop in Mountjoy Prison: Women's Wing

The small screw
of the white stride
and no passion
rings with keys
as she skirts
the outrage of the flower bed.

A bed of roses between two walls

Ruby lips
bunned hair
round thighs
Screw her in the dark
of who'd be you
they say.

A bed of roses between two walls

Hello, screw
will you give us a sigh
like the thin light
that whispers into the cell
caresses the chair
the table—the confused
thoughts in the copy-book.

A bed of roses between two walls

The sun shines through rain—
they call it a monkey's wedding
a gathering beyond the bars
is it two hundred feet
by thirty once a day?

A bed of roses between two walls

The Song of the Saw

That winter they fell in love
over the cross cut
In their white silence
the hills enclosed them

It was the bitter winter of '47
when people died of hypothermia
No trains ran—bread was short
Sounds were fragments of sound
the whisper of the feathers of a bird
the distant crunch of a boat
They caught each other's smiles
above the zing of the saw
as the logs split and fell
Into the sawdust.

The Cross Cut

That winter they fell in love
over the cross cut
that bitter winter of '47
when the country slept
under a stretched white canvas.

No bird called that winter
only the saw's song
was the persistent nudging
of the earth.

Raven

Poe wasn't daft. That great bird,
lonesome, yet
with wife, he dwelt
above Lough Dan
always the one pair.
Superior, barely deigning
to look our way
they'd made home
a perch, without title or lease

Raven, pride of place
beyond the bracken
above the sharp scars
coarsened and blackened
by Wicklow winds
Above the dark pool where
no sun shines
that was their haven.
No human dared
that fearsome climb
But as a child I marvelled
at this faith wherein
reason lived; yes, reason
forevermore.

Mrs Russell

Our greatest childhood moments
were those we spent with Mrs Russell
in her small red car we packed ourselves
squashed limbs, tobacco clogged
smoke drawn in, in great relaxing gulps
the days were ours, all ours.

We fondled swear-words
the ones that roll and trip—
those dark sequestered nouns
forbidden in our kitchens
like 'shit' and 'cunt', both stark and clipped
and how we laughed, oh how we laughed.

Dear God, every child, but every child
should have a Mrs Russell.

The Single Voice in the Night

It breaks through
to the cox-orange colour
The rich knowing that there is
something called wonder
on the bridge of years

"Come, come,
you are welcome." But not
the bitter heart
of tragedy—it leans like a tired man
over the doubt of laughter
because the corded tears
play hide and seek
with the continual change
of season's colours.

The Day I Knew

When the day scratched in
In November '01
a Thursday, I think, and
as sure as I'm sitting here
I knew.
So I says

I was lenient towards the piano
That day. Sheets
of Debussy, and Granados
unlikely bedfellows, ribbed
at my feet. I had bargained for
at least another year.

from

The Noise of Masonry Settling

(Dedalus Press, 2006)

The Knowledge of Beezie McGowan

She knows where the whelks gather,
the booty of waves,
the mussels.

She knows where the limpets lie,
how the rocks
are spreading.

She knows where the dillisk hides
in the pitted cracks
when the water's ebbing.

She can tell the storm
by the heron's flight
from cliff to harbour,

But wages were poor
in this industry of God's,
the learning got so hard, so hard.

‘These Aspirins Seem to Be No Use’—

Last Words of Ernest Shackleton, died of Angina Pectoris, January 4th, 1922

for my cousin Robbie

What possessed you
on that last trip, sucking on the fags,
drinking champagne by the neck,
imagining your poor heart
Could get you there and back?

As your heart couldn’t follow,
you followed it
like all great explorers—
Emily Brontë, saying
‘You can send for the doctor now,’
Tolstoy, doing press-ups
at the railway station,
Flaubert wishing
he hadn’t written *Madame Bovary*…

Maybe it’s the pure whiteness
the spirit needs
that drives one on in the end.

Hard to Imagine Your Face Dead

Hard to imagine your face dead,
not giving out, pontificating,
just quiet, serene, the moustache resting
over the broken tooth.

Those eyes—no longer
like water brimming
over a gutter caught with sun.

Your shoulders, no longer alert
in your cushion of death,
their anger subsiding.

Better to imagine you lying
alone and listless,
like when the speed used to leave you
in the downbeat of your madness.

Where the Grass Is Dark With Trees

for Dan

I want to walk in the field
where the grass is dark with trees

I want to take the hand of the past
as round and clean as an autumn apple

and hold it tight as a nail
till all the talking is done

For the seabird's cry is still the saddest

Oh Well! (De Mortuis… etc)

Climbing the spinal steps,
the vertebraic ladder,
the fieldmouse of panic
creeps silently

In the heel of night,
the skin of her anger
racing from terminal to terminal,
dodging and doubling back
from the campanology
of the mortuary doors.

Gráinne dragging fishtails
to the mountain cave.

The West's Asleep

Death comes handy, they say,
when the leaf snaps,
sleeps and stalks back,
when the bud quickens.
Two months that bring up the toll.

As the years pass
the houses empty.
No light shines from the windows,
no dogs bark on the long road
that hangs from Cloonagh.

A straggling beard
of ragweed, thistle, goosefoot,
and the wild cup of the rose
calls out the names:
Tom, The Black Doctor,
Ellie, Sarah, Jack.
Ah sure,
they're all gone now
and none to come after.

That Day

Either
Darryl F. Zanuck or
Cecil B. DeMille
said, *I employed*
Gary Cooper
the day
he got old.

Can ordinary people,
who are not
film directors
recognise that day
without being told?

My Brother Reggie

My brother Reggie
was generous with epithets—
Face-Ache, Vim Tin, Toast-Rack—
not without a trace
of humour. Why not let
me be Maid of the Track?
I asked. It did not
crack his face.

My brother Reggie
liked to put the pillow
over my head, and press,
press down so
till my head was flat.
He said, *I want you dead*.
But what fun is there in that?

My Brother Reggie,
a gentleman to his guts,
is a hundred years old
and hedges his bets.
He doesn't care to put
his hands round my throat
and squeeze me weird.
Like a goat,
he just hugs his beard.

Love Poem

The nicest thing
you ever said to me
was
Do we always have to live
like Bonnie and Clyde?

The Night's Empty Shells

I am always afraid
they will find me
like the skinned arm of the child,

Break the joint between
the ulna and the radius,
gouge out the mephitic matter,

Take the dance from my feet,
splay the small bones,
work the cement into the instep
before I have settled the measure.

I am not here to ogle the sea,
count the Brent geese,
on the short strand below Ardtrasna,

I'm here to learn the light of Lislary
where shone the shebeen once:
a fisherman's star.

So sailed Praeger
after breakfast of poitín
and cold potatoes—a note

to the waves—a leaky boat,
a nod to the dawn
on the East of Inishmurray.

For once on my gable
a beacon shone,
the end of the sea lane

To a safe hauling
of the night's empty shells.

Heart Trouble

It was the heart, after all,
that let her down.
So she lay under the frown
of the cardiologist,
thinking:
at least this is respectable.
It might have been me found
dead drunk in someone else's kitchen.

Inishmurray

'Where there's a cow there's a woman and where there's a woman, there's mischief'

—St Colmcille who founded the monastery
and banned all cows from the island

Two thumb holes in the birthing stone
beside the women's graveyard.

There she squats, prayers
breaking from parched lips

to the great Man-God to deliver her
from the yearly gall of labour,

to beg for a man-child
to erase the guilt of her sex.

For being a woman
has no pardon,

skirts raised in the wind
on an island that floats

like a bayleaf
in the unforgiving sea.

She crouches thus
till the infant lies in the scutch

and she looks at the unmarked grave
beneath whose soil her mother lies.

She ponders.

'No Road Beyond the Graveyard'

—Chief Inspector Morse in a novel by Colin Dexter

But the No Road beyond the graveyard
is full of possibilities,
eidetic visions, ghosts,
The valedictory sigh, perhaps.
But when I stand on this No Road,
I am thinking of an old woman
who took the shoes of her son
and polished them, polished them,
till you could see your face in them,
first the left, then the right,
and placed them under the kitchen table
before she died. And the son
stands at the No Road
in the dulled shoes,
in a hopeless frame of mind.
There's no reason for this No Road.
No mention of falling stones,
dangerous cliffs
likely to flood.
Simply No Road,
no five-barred gate,
no 'Dogs Keep Out',
no 'Danger Men at Work',
no 'Closed for Repair',
just, beyond the graveyard,
'No Road'.
No cul de sac, no boreen
no bridle path.
The road doesn't go nowhere,
it simply isn't.
It's quiet too in the graveyard
no creature, no bird,
no field mouse. Quiet.
Rows upon rows of stones
crosses, inscriptions, dates,
but quiet. In the end
one keeps one's ghosts
to oneself.

Hawthornden Castle

These forces on the battlements
make snakes pass through her bloodstream.
lecherous ghosts torment her
with the hooting
of the distant owl. She cannot sleep
on this moonlit plain
to the ticking of the Rosewell mine,
the town ill-named with its stumpy streets,
mean houses pasted over
with a coal-dust sheen.
She remembers, too, the hedgehog,
lifeless, lying
like a discarded gardener's glove.

Drum up a Poem

Drum up a poem,
they said, *for Eddie's birthday*,
and me as empty as
an upturned barrel.

Who then is this
Aquarius fellow,
this Eddie Linden?
is he some sort
of astronaut
in the bend of the wind
that the poor folks
like us remember
who did demons for us
as we struggled to climb
on to the empty page?

Good luck, so.

To the beat
of your Irish
Scottish heart
from this upturned barrel
I send you
a drum of delight.

Cherry Blossom Again

Cherry blossom falls again
from the tree. Spring
has drifted away and old age
drags around me.
Why did sense pass me by
without a primrose of recognition?

Will I never emerge from the reel
of the ring, till the enchanted earth
smiles cynically?
Will the mist always hide the garden from me?

Old People's Outing: Ageism

The old man on the telly
at the old people's outing
was smiling but not breathing.
He was dressed in women's clothes.

The compère had dressed all the old men
in women's clothes,
rolled up their pants to expose
their soiled long-johns.
Fun, they yelled loudly.
This is real fun, they cackled
to keep the shudder of death away
But the one old man
Smiled hopelessly.
He had, for the last time,
made a fool of himself.

Block

To beat the block
she painted dried flowers,
baked bread,
put wine in the borscht,
read *Finnegans Wake*,
but still her mind was as flat as Hungary.
"I need to fall in love,
I need pain," she cried,
"real pain.
Not just bad news on the telephone."

The Lady Who Went on Strike Outside the Iveagh Hostel Because of Its Early Closing Hours

I am Lily, comfy, leave
me alone. My daft umbrellas
shelter me. My mattress
shapes my bones.

You can have old pin-
stripe and his lock-up
face in the Iveagh.

Why should I snuff
his candle light
and blow his dandelion clock?
The Liberties is my domain.
My carpet runs from Thomas Street
to St. Nicholas Without.

I lie here from Monday to Sunday.
My street's my Alphabet Walk.
I have a God-room
on this leaning street and
love on my tree like ivy.
I am Lily, comfy, live or die.

Ghost Child Runs

The top of my house succumbed to fire,
slates lie where they fell,
a bay window at the side
swings on one hinge
like the tongue of a famine child.
The room I slept in staggers
under the ceiling-weight of rubble.
I can feel the noise of masonry settling
as the fire raced through its innards—
with casualties of floor
and ceiling, joist and window frame.

I burrow through basement
and drawing room—cyclamen wallpaper
shrouds my shoulders or falls dog-eared
into folds of heavy dust.
Two bats flash past—a spitting sound,
the radar of childhood quickens.

Going back (home) after forty years
may be a mistake, for now
the tall bay horse, coat dark as wine,
stands, straddle-legged on the gravel.
A short walk to the spent wood
that runs crooked into the stream
beyond Durkin's yard… The tall horse
stamps its unshod hooves
like gloved hands knocking
on the powdery wood
of the old hall door. Mr. Durkin
too, is long long dead—a man for books,
no time to tie his laces
or straighten his aching back.
Ghost horse, ghost man, ghost child runs.

The Grave Digger

He came, saying
"keep it Country",
Clint Eastwood riding
the stacks. "It smells sweet
up here in the cemetery."

He said, "Neighbour,
I'm country,
and that's the seventh dug.
It's a bad November."

He came into the pit,
earth and all. They took
the mule-train fast
the wires zinged,
a gorse fire raged.
"No putting it out
in this class of wind
though it's from the West and sweet."

Morning she heard the horse
shake its bit, the harness clang.
She wondered about the sea,
would the star-cold water
Suffice to cool her thighs?

A Paean for My Uncle Kit Who Died Before I Was Born

What did you think of
all those years
pegging away in the mines?

Just a little short of breath,
you wrote, a touch of miner's
phthisis, nothing much

after seven years below.
Many men die after three,
that's what you wrote

from Benoni, Transvaal
in 1917 and three years later,
you were dead.

The price of diamonds fell,
and you all went out on strike
What was it? A drunken brawl?

Did you hit your head
on the edge of the pavement?
Did someone say:

"What's he doing there
lying in the muck?"
An old young man of thirty -five,

Why did you go to Africa to die?
What did they tell you, your family?
That you were too wild

too dangerously wild
for their Protestant
mores? Too eccentric?

Did you tell them, "So I'll go
seek my fortune elsewhere
if I'm a nuisance here."

The Black sheep dragging
the family down,
did you embarrass them

with your curly locks
so beautifully portrayed
by Orpen when you were a boy.

You were full of wonder then,
as later you must have been
all those years so far from home,

Those seven long years
in the dark African tunnels,
wondering what brought you there.

But you took your wonder with you
nearly as far as man can go
and closed the book on it.

They didn't write to you.
They tore up all your letters.
Only a single one survived.

You were my favourite uncle
although we never met.
Your face plays on the lute

of my imagination,
the one friend out of all
I might have had.

Bag Lady

I knew her when she was a bag lady.
She trundled places like the North Circular Road,
O'Connell Street and Fairview,
followed the Liffey, a restless bone,
lay down under the lid of Clery's.
But when she knew the eyes of the orphans
had left her, she folded her briefcase
and took the long dark highway
that had always beckoned.

Barnacles

Irish Sea north westerly 7 or 8
increasing 10 for a time
Shannon Rockall northerly
increasing north backing northwest
Dogger Cromarty Viking
Malin Hebrides.
Doors bang, buckets race
down the field, my skirt
wraps round me
like a sari. Gulls lift
and scatter like paper.
A boat bobs like a bead
as a shoulder lifts
and rolls in with a shrug.
And then the thrash of wings.
It is six o'clock, the island calls,
and the geese face into the gale,
a cardiograph in the sky . . .

Insomnia

With me in my truckle bed
there is a hound
a hound in my head
there is no gainsaying it
it howls

It is the lessons of darkness

Oh Couperin
Couperin Le Grand

Pigeon outside the Dead Woman's House

Like a casual passer-by
she strolls, her shawl
of feathers neatly pinned.

Outside Theresa's cottage
she picks at the crumbs
of the old woman's soul.

Maybe takes it on loan.
When life peters out like that
there's no certainty

of who is who, whether
Theresa is the pigeon
or the pigeon is Theresa.

It is true that Theresa,
when still living,
gazed at the island,

the island of her birth
perhaps thinking
were I a bird

I'd give it a peck,
a peck of a kiss,
just there and back.

So maybe the pigeon
is just hanging around
for instructions.

First published in *Ambit* as "Hound"

Magherow Movements

He repeated the word *Duvet*
as though it were a charm.
Duvet, he said, curling his socks
around her feet.

The Invisible from the USA to Iraq

We are too late again.
We have to get our bearings
in the gutter.

The sky is dark.
The birds assemble—
a murder of crows.

We dream of justice
where a pride of lawyers
tumbles through our brains.

We must take action, we say,
against the invisible.
It thinks it has us trapped.

It likes to set pipebombs
for unsuspecting children
as it shouts out loudly:

"She's only a girl-woman
crying on the sofa."

The Song of the Whale

And the whale beached
in Lislary. And they brought the JCB
and buried it. All thirty foot of it.
They said it was black,
shining skin from the sea.
Grey blue, some argued
all thirty foot of it.
And the whale men came,
they came all the way from Cork,
for that is where the whale men
and the dolphin men hang out,
and they made their notes
and ecological plans and took
blood samples and measured the tide
so that the whale now lies
under the limestone reaches,
proud steps to the summer storm,
turquoise and shimmering,
great sea mammal, partner of song.

S.A.D.

Winter is icummen in, / Lhude sing Goddamm

—Ezra Pound

The swallows pack up
and go.
Tomorrow the geese
will come.
Inside the house
in the purple dark
the table
with its city of junk
tells you
that winter leans on you,
has nudged you through all
the tower and babel
of the past months
when a kind of summer
was. Now the table tells you
it's the S.A.D.
Stale bread, hard as a helmet,
dregs of tea, the last teabag
like a dead mouse,
yesterday's
half-finished crossword,
tells you
it's for winter.

Who's for winter?
says your man
below, growing his house.

The Horse Protestant Joke is Over

There's a small church
by the Big House
outside of which
the notice reads
Everyone welcome.

Two grinning
millionaires
have bought the Big House

And they will have horses,
and they will have jeeps,
and maybe ride rough-shod
over the parishioners
of the little church
which says
Everyone welcome.

House for Sale

for Sophia McColgan

Still the house stands
in its rope of wind,
small cenotaph
to the weeds of evil,
the stone of memory
a solid fortress
that time
will not erase.

The children's voices
under chair and wardrobe,
between the cracks
in the lino . . .
The broken hinge of terror
in the swinging door
that swings over and over
is the house's destiny

Till it crumbles in history
unwanted, unsold.

Song

I gave a poem to my friend.
He spat upon the burning ground.
I said, *My friend, it's not the end,*
my song is better than it sounds.
But he said lately he had found
that matter divulged and matter penned
created enemies all around.

I wrapped my poem up in lead
and threw it in his scarlet face.
I said, *My friend, I wish you dead*
for such a terrible disgrace.
But then he only laughed instead
and wrapped his Easter up in lace.

In the Out-Patients of St Mary's Hospital, on the Eve of Good Friday Last

High on Reds, short for Seconal,
drunk out of her person,
bumming fags—beautiful lady
of London wept for the crucified Lord.
He died for us, for me, for you,
transfigured, tomorrow we'll toast Him with whiskey.
The casualty's slack lips tightened.
Her words, encrusted with slime and sentiment,
banged the air like a fist.
She wept. She crossed herself.
Tears from her crazy Calvary—
The prescription got would rise again
in Wigmore Street—
the all-night drug-addicts' haven.
Perfection is easily gained.
Social Security pays—legal high,
suicide, bets on the Derby—you name it.
She was foul-mouthed, loving and highly practical.

‘The Act of Poetry Is a Rebel Act’

—*Michael Hartnett*

Possibly those inquisitive eyes
grasped the horizon
of his wonder gift,
tell-tales of lift-the-heart
follies—like addressing the statue
in Kiltimagh of a brandy-shadowed
morning: *No wars of mercy fought*
on his behalf. His waging, lonesome
as any poet’s, playing the poker
of ‘See you, raise you’ till its echo tumbled
from the kitty of common sense.
How well he knew
‘The act of poetry
is a rebel act.’

Precisely

Of course
all things are rich to me.
Precision, equally, is correct.
The muscles of a boy's back
in early Latin sun,
The line of a Bentley tourer
parked in a Georgian square,
not to mention the neck
of a racehorse,
money itself,
the ablative absolute,
white in the sun,
the cold of a cathedral,
the smell of a new tennis ball,
Couperin's *Leçons de ténèbres . . .*

Still, I have seen
the boy, the Bentley
and the racehorse.
I have felt money and the cold
of a cathedral,
have smelled the new tennis ball
and heard Couperin's
Leçons de ténèbres.

But memory games
make patches wear
in the heart.

This is a variant version of the earlier poem 'Precisement'

Four Woodbines

In the torn and dirty sheets of those winter years
spent in my wet mac, clutching the green packet
with its fiery orange sash—four Woodbines—
and my mongrel dog scratching its pedigree of fleas,
I was happy as a child could be, hiding under the shelf of Confey.

Drunk from the spilling rain, the stumpy field
shrank from the ruined church, the glue factory,
four headstones, I remember, aslant and broken as winos.

The winter mists came early then,
tucked up the river in a long white scarf

While, heavy with fish and water-hens,
it rolled on quietly in the textured night.

Twopence halfpenny—old money—
not much to pay in retrospect
for the healing wonder of that glorious leaf.

This is a variant of the poem 'Confey'

Nightmare

It is dark in my father's shoe,
his experienced shoe. I scratch my skin
on the buckle and the laces.

He crunches about
on top of me. Underneath his arm

he has a cricket bat.
He is waiting
for the next man out.

A Mother Mourns Her Heroin-Addicted Daughter

How could I have dreamt
that my bird of paradise,
my green-clad hippie girl,
could be so reduced
to the gammon face of poverty,
the incessant whinge of a child.

If we rolled up time like a ball
I'd give you the cherries of my nipples,
I'd wash you almond clean
and lay your hair like lint
on the cartilage of my breast.

A prey to the barren street, you're lost
on the breach of years that no silk
nor cotton drawing-to of threads
can mend. The void. Your path is marked
like gull-prints on an empty beach.

The drug has perished your will.
You float like a stick on a pond
in here, in there—to a harbour of lily-trees,
or held for days in scum till the light
breeze lifts you and you edge along.

Will you walk on my street once more?
I'll raise my pavements to keep you safe,
open the balcony of my arms.
I will buckle your shoes again
and shine the mirror for your dance.

But you will not throw away your bag of tricks.
Your monkey fingers cling to the safety net
in which you nightly land, having walked
the trembling wire and heard the screams
of anticipation, seen the up-turned mouths.

How can we meet down the glaciers
of days, the furnaces of nights?

The Violets of the Poor

My muse invites me to forget my debts,
pile up more enemies.

Invoke the few

who are helpful, generous
but not always honest.
To make secrets for the few
like "whispering time".

But the few are filtered
and numbered in the funerals.
They follow the coffins.

So I pacify my muse
by joining the cortège
and sprinkling my secrets to the mourners
like the violets of the poor.

Black in Achill

What makes black so black?
Black soul, black Protestant
black widow, black cat,
black holes, black death.
So many blacks in Achill:
Dugort, Dooagh, Dooega
Dookinella. Black field,
black land, black plain.
But what if, like a camera click,
the sun comes out
and shadows scythe
the mountain's umber skin
and gorse-gold sand?

Poems in Periodicals & from Bardwell's Papers

DNA

for Jonas, Jesse and Dan

Now that my youngest children
are pushing forty
it's time to open the account,
how much do I owe each one
for surviving the swinging doors
of my neglect

When each child came
the black tail of my mother's
hatred baulked and blemished
my abilities, my genuine desire
not to repeat the rallentando
of her cruelties.

She with her painter's hands
her desperate inhibitions
darkened the landscape of my intelligence
left me thick and muted
wits astray, imagining
that never having handled love
love would spring for you
like a genie from a bottle

Too late to apologise
to say, forgive me—I made
a holy hames of rearing you.
Too late to say I didn't love you
enough, bluff my way
to redemption, to get a purchase
on the sloping
roof of my life

Too late to say, I love you now
fiercely and dangerously
like the sun, the sea and the wind
As though to hang Death up
on a hook, an unworn coat,
too smart, too fresh
from the tailor.
A garment I haven't earned.

Now that you in turn
are parents and will want
to 'do it right'
can the DNA of chance
halt for even a moment
while you catch your breath?
Can the poisoned cargo
of your childhood
slip from the dock
a flotilla of broken promises.

Colours

Sometimes I dream of blue
as pale as the underside
of a pigeon's wing
or the greeny grey of moonlight
grass, or that subtle Florentine stone
like baked corn bread.
If only I could paint
I would take my dream for a walk
and set it free.

Council Proposes €75 Fine for Breach of Beach Laws

I'll go down to the beach
horseless, carless, dogless
I'll go alone with the moon
Light no fire for my soul,

I'll take no alcohol
keep no caravan, no tent
seat, chair, notice board,

Nor will I call a meeting,
have a party, attract a crowd.
I'll play no golf, I promise,
no small ball will spin
its dangerous course on the sand,
I'll go down to the beach alone.

Cloonagh Grows

Every day a new one;
diggers dancing, twirling
their petticoats, hefty
unwieldy creatures
like women from other
oceans. The Atlantic slyly
turns the other cheek.

To make more space
they cut the whins
hurling the bushes
on the ground. Like
one would hurl a shawl

Rivers of mud gulp
down the gulleys
all is squash
and squelch.
All pass warily, picking
footholds one by one
as the kestrel picks his prey

We glow now
with bigness
us Irish. Say: "Fuck you Jack,"
we keel round in our glory.
Selling the famine ruins
for money heavy got

In the bend of the bay
lovely Cloonagh grows.
Takes pride of place
in the planet's altered spin.

Islands

I asked a famous painter once,
"Why do you not paint horses?"
And his answer was
"Because they are so beautiful."

"But so are Islands," I said
He laughed sadly, saying "yes,
I know."

*

Tears

The doctor has flowers
everywhere
on his desk the notes
of incurable tragedies
are smothered in flowers
perhaps the birds
who maybe twirled their beaks
harsh with squawks
as the leaf might break
and the small wise eye
might wink; brass bold
would hop from branch
to petal—petal to leaf
till the doctor is finally safe
his eyes are dry.

Each flower holds the tear's
reflection, the tear's pain
the doctor, quiet now
with head bold slant at last
heaven held, sinks silently
among the curling leaves.

Ugly as Sin

Like Lucia Joyce
I'm frightened of my nose
I powder it
in front of the dead T.V.

*

80 Year Old Lady

The eightieth birthday
is like a barbed wire fence
If you can crawl under it
without snagging your clothes
you're lucky.

*

Snow

The notice in my local shop says
Sorry!
No More Credit.
I look the shop-owner in the eye.
She looks back at me,
Silent as the snow.

The House That Jack Built

Tiers
Her house is so small
it's all in tiers
like acrobats
things balance
on top of each other.
The woman rises
at four a.m.
to kneel in the grate
to make pyramids of coal
Tidying up the tiers
ready for Jack
to tell her
how wonderful he is.

Friends at the Rubbish Dump

Here's where we hurl
our passions,
tell the story of
all we keep, clutch
onto—flotsam of longing
The might-come-ins
of a life that's nearly there

Wherewith our peccadilloes
confessed—like: "Daddy
I stole a half a crown
for fags from your jacket
yesterday—I'm sorry?"

But the detritus,
not heavy things,
like sins or guilt or learning
Only the charts
of memory, the spiders webs
of hearts so torn, they're
misted off by the constant toil
of "The knitters in the sun . . ."

But the bottles
of what we did not do
will be recycled over and over
into shards of glass
that even with
pin-prick accuracy
can't be extracted.

Crossing the Brow

Perhaps I do not need
to cross the brow
of the tall mountain after all.
Need not look up any more
instead I can board the train
that crosses far countries
and carries the laughter of those
who had to leave early.

Taking the sweet drug of poppies
the transient songs of adolescence
that ring in your head
the ten o'clock summer evenings
of His Master's Voice with
the dog that looks so mournfully
into the horn of the wind-up gramophone.

This I must not mourn, for this
is as the snipe crossing the bog.
That is his business—his speed
his element, as I must accept mine
as the curragh accepts
the turbulence of the sea.

Room

Only when you've lost your room
do you know the meaning of room
which isn't only space.
Only when you owned a room
and you've just found out
what your room had meant
do you understand loss.

So outside my room
which is no longer my room
I walk the river again
till tears block my breathing
as I remember the garden
outside my room
and below the garden
a man kissing a horse.

Seven Rings

in memory of Steffi

She rang me seven times,
the dying woman.

Seven dying rings
on my answering machine

Seven times calling my name
yet I was not there to hear her.

My name suspended in the air
will float there forever

she wanted me to hold
her voice in the air

so as the air would keep it for her
but she went, holding my name

as the thorn holds the web
the spider has woven.

My Belief in Summer

for Jesse

June, and I have the fire lit
while the thin wind
creaks around my house
Yet I am not nonplussed
for somewhere there's
a puzzle of brightness.

The ballerinas dancing
in the fuchsia, the paintbrush
in the leaf of the hebe

So my belief in summer
may be justified

The Dancer

It’s my fault; I gave you everything
Thanks. I stay.
With a quick sideways glance
that’s how the dance ends
The dancer must stand still
for the vampire. Music
fills the roof.

It’s my fault. I gave you nothing
Thanks. I go now.
With a quick sideways glance.
That’s how the dance ends
The vampire will catch the dancer
on his way out. Music
fills the roof.

Mother, Mer—Seal Sequence

I
Slithering on your limestone reaches
I face you, Mother, I know your tricks
you threw me out
to eat humble pie
to those who'll steal my pelt
that's the kind they are
and not say thanks.

Now on this dry-as-dust earth
I grind my trade
honing and scratching
tearing the golden sods
but my body's tired
Please stop this growling and cursing,
thumping, dragging, showing off
your superior skill, your cunning
If only you'd tell me
what you want, still want from me
but you won't
and I won't compromise

II
I am the keeper of the rocks,
I sit because it's easier,
my body's tired
it leans towards the horizon
where the storm
lives with my mother.
My mother lifts
and crashes at my feet.

I tell her
I am the keeper of the rocks
and linger here
to watch my mother recede
gathering up these nestlings

My children huddle
in my mother's arms
as she humps and pulls
them from me
I watch them go to my mother.
Mother, I cry, don't take them
but she crashes back at my feet

Dragging and crashing and dragging
I sit because it's easier
I am the keeper of the rocks.

III
We can't always blame you, mother
lying like a faithful friend
who would one day leave us
shrugging and retreating
until all our loves and cares
are taken from us
telling us in the way you do
how much better off
we are without.

Is it because you are
lying up your sleeve
trying to convince us
that you know best
with a convincing calm
you pull away as far
as the stones-drag takes you
so as you can stay quiet and wait.

IV
So mother,
you are always there
no matter how I slide away
or work into the gullies,
crouch in the limestone
to hide from your fury
but your anger ebbs; and flows
as only you know how.

All my life I have tried
to measure your distance,
your strength, and find
what you first gave me
You must know.
From you I came
you must remember.
Or is the cliff slant
so steep and the crashing
of time too hidden
that even the smallest ripple
is shrugged away?

Please tell me mother
with your great strength,
and beauty, that there must be time.
Formed and quiet
against the thin reflective sky
the silent strip of snow
hides the wet bog that time
owns—time alone owns.

Must it always be like this, then?
Amongst the uncombed tangle of reeds
that time lies like a sheet
and in its way has no time for us.
It's the absolute stillness that matters
and even if the planet
turned upside down at an angle
there'd be snow-silence
and then the footsteps:
Whither? Why?
All we see is absence.

V
Now, Mother
you think you have us fooled
with your flat apron of water
a table top of quiet
and the purity of blue
What is this message?
Is this the quiet before storm?
A hurricane of anger
boiling up out there

A terrible fear attacks me
I want my children near
because you will snatch them
like you did once before
taking their love from me
So as I lie here loveless
no love to give
since you have shorn me
like you would a sheep his wool

Where can I turn? Is there any hope?
Or must I always carry a kind of guilt?
The terrible pain that sears my chest
and makes a creature of me
shamefully weakened in will.
A loss to my kind
Hear me, mother, I beg you
Listen.

VI
I must apologise, please, to them,
Mother, before you take my children
Take them away in the hugeness
of your skirts. They must be told, how sorry
I am—they must know, Mother
and if I know they know, Mother
only then my heart will rest.
Rest on your limestone reaches
to the sough of the wind. Or the hurricane
you like so much. I will hide beneath
the boulders and even as you crash
and pull and try to drag me off
they will be there with my sorrow
and will not need me. Mother
please leave me now

Counties

I sit here counting counties
as though I was in a game
especially Kildare—the short grass county
I feel that special grass, lime hidden
as it curls among my fingers

Why do I have to count them?
North and West
Why not let them sleep?
Stripping my mind
like the taking off of a bandage—yes
it hurts, I cannot leave them
they are mine. I want
to gather them in my arms
lay my head among their leaves.

Old age paring my brain
as the stops and starts of folly
I have lost the time—twisted,
jostled, wasted, crushed, rejected,
slaughtered. Like my son,
who saw the jaguar pacing,
said, "He does not know which way".

Pain

The pain in my bones
is as hollow as an old shoe.
When I wake each day I imagine
Death is having me on
as though to tantalise me
and share the joke
with all the others out there.

Yes, a tantalising forerunner
of something much much worse.
As if to say "you think this is bad?
Just try and walk. Then you'll
have something to complain about."

So. "Is there a name for this pain?"
I ask, adding, "don't get into a tantrum."
But Death can't be bothered to answer,
uses a monstrous laugh
to wipe the skin off my face
I have nothing to say except, "Please."

No Tragedy

We are thinking very hard
and trying to work out
a place where the sea
will rejoice on its luck
and lie quiet.

I'll walk with that vivid smile
I was once praised for

Then my acceptance
of the heartbreak
will breach out the tragedies,
and stoutly accept the question:
what are they?

Just Go

They will try to
send me to the place
where women lie silently
and in rows.

One would wonder
why women could be so
stupid? Obedient?
Hopeful?
What, in the name of God,
do they expect to achieve?
To print in their minds
this "will to live"
rather than "just go!"

So we, poor creatures
want to "hang in"
and for what?
To have some bored-stiff helper
clean you up in the morning
and light your fire?

Other early poems

Fable

A man organised a life
believing all the world's a stage etc.,
but went one step forward
being a good stage manager.
he created neo-strindbergian intrigues
In order to sit back and watch them snowball.

Once he went too far;
tripped up and fell into the snow;
knowing but not being
had hitherto been his forte.
Suddenly trapped
he shouted for friends;
but the actors all ran away
to commit suicide.

The make-up man and the stage-hands
were much too busy to attend
to the weakest link in his armour.

The End of the Party

Most of the guests had gone
she heard the taxi meters click;
on the floor Dick, Harry, Tom
were lying down and looking sick;
another marathon party done,
she stood there smiling half alone
"Oh, my darlings you are ill"
"You'll sleep with me tonight?" they said,
she, acquiescing, sighed, "I will
no other love but yours will suit me quite as well"

Dick, Tom and Harry moaned,
stirring in alcoholic dreams,
to murmur the Golden Sounds,
(how sure the whole thing seems)
and when all is said and shuffling words
No longer carry weight;
like music that goes on in thirds,
each view becomes opinionate;
"The drink's the whore" they said;
she, acquiescing, sighed, "I'm sure;
no other love but yours would suit me quite as well."

Words upon Golden Words were said,
(How Scott Fitzgerald had foreseen.
MacAndrew's Hymn, Tom often read,
and Harry April 1916.
With "A Rosebud by the Early Walk"
Dick broke the flights of omniscient talk).
And as Tom, Dick and Harry stirred
their bloodshot alcoholic eyes,
"Love," they cried, "Love is the Word,"
she acquiescing, sighed "It is;
no other love but yours would suit me quite as well."

"But all is lost," they said,
"We use big symbols like the seas
that toss and drown our measured fate,
but it's only dawn that drowns

the electric bulbs; and the day is slow
for love is as slow in withering
as leaves that gather late.
She acquiescing, sighed "I know;
no other love but yours would suit me quite as well."

Then she must choose her bed-mate last,
to hurt the least the nicest one,
for her, there's nothing left to lose,
for her, no future, only past
ambition struggling on;
an elephant that treads on glass.
Stretch out to them one thin arm
so that their hearts should know no harm.
"Once more," she sighed, "I must have kept
a vigil for you while you slept.
No other love but yours would suit me quite as well."

The girl got up and made the tea
with lots of sugar. "Think of me,
I've got 2,000 words to write
before the post goes out tonight.
For every day it is the same
I'm fed up with La Vie de Bohème.
Is it possible I've spent
Every single single cent?
Oh God, how can we all endure
Another day without a cure?"
"But" she reminded, "Love is the cause"
"How can you expect to pause?"
"No other love but yours would suit me quite as well."

London 1960

Lament

I knew that once I was dependent
my love for you would be redundant.

I knew a pretty girl would take
my love away for true love's sake.
Sick with remorse and sick with pain,
I asked my true love back again.
A snarl and elegant shrug was all
I got for my fretful begging call.

"I do not want your sad dejection,
not even your care and your protection,
I merely want a little peace
to follow up my own device!"

And all my friends who are so nice
now bludgeon me with their advice
"You do not need this Casanova
when you can have me as a lover!"

So I cut again and cut the decks,
(there is no substitute for sex)
alas I cannot save my face;
I cannot cut the God-damned ace!

A Prayer for All Young Girls

Dear God, make me sophisticated
Dear God, make me highly equipped;
Dear God, make me easily bored,
not tolerant, hard-working, energetic,
not sober nor militant
Dear God, make me rich, taxi-minded, expeditious,
vicious at the right times.
Make me please, dear God,
a thorough-going sex-ridden bitch. Amen.

And a Nursery Rhyme for All Girls

Little Miss Tepid
Sat on a virgin,
praying for Prince Charming.

Along came a tortoise
who said "Baby you're no hare!"
But Miss Tepid wasn't with it.

Portrait

Although the first to arrive,
were yet the last to leave;
over-enthusiastic, much too gay,
you could betray
years of friendship
for a moment's laughter.

In that light, destructive,
do not dare
to claim the slightest tolerance;
"You have sung all summer, dance
now!" How can you share
the outline of a mountain
from the empty empty Sunday streets
in their crepuscular glory?

It is another story
That in the course of time
all innocence is known
and God decides the runners;
the flag falls softly at the 'off.'
Who are you to moan?

At Another Birthday Party

Your face, undisturbed as a nun's
watched our appreciation
as record after record unfolded
your links with an emotional past.
At last it ended!

We commended your extraordinary
knowledge and taste.
On the other hand what waste
of energy expended
on one singer (some thought).

The recipient of the present
blandly accepted the shift of shrine
and with calm and charm extended
his hands to the giver.

Being clever you restored our status
with champagne, dispensing confidence and gaiety
the laity were not exactly bored
but had had their egos restrained;
we needed the temporary hiatus.

Summer 1964

The sun, which we are not used to
has been shining the whole season through;
as I gather sticks in the unusual warmth
of the night, the night owl hoots
but that's not all, the lonely ass
like its city counter-part,
whose only reason for living
is giving its company to
a thoroughbred,
raises its head the once
and brays.

But the book I'm reading says:
"Les dames des quartiers
distingués—ô Jésus—Les malades du foie
font baisers doigt jaunes aux bénitiers."
Yet I must return with my sticks
my way was fixed like a star
that's seen through a hole in the wall
to my fireside, which is neither church nor hall
nor any kind of worship place;
just a hot hearth on an August night
with a trace of what imparts
a wistful possibility of that.

Quiet, like Baucis and Philemon
we two just sat.

Star

Twinkle twinkle mad star of the poet
that mocks the shivering critics
jostling for places at Coward's Gate.
The guttering candle flame has claimed
the quantities of their tongue.

And the young tree
will stand dead in the dark
its bark and nervous system hacked
by the fangs of the mordant ferret.

The Lady Knew More Than Most

Tempted to win, the lady knew more than most,
one morning she woke up bored
(he hadn't the ghost of a chance)
when sex and pity shared
the bed of arrogance.

The truth comes by mouth only
and the hungry tongue cries its salt tears
for more and more. We must try
to curb our voluptuous wishes
to a more ascetic lie.

Portrait of a Pub

Effete shadows meet,
throwing aside Mephistophelian capes
of virility.

Words of incredible vanity escape
yesterday's mouths.
Occasionally a couth lawyer
stealthily passes through.

Men from the clothing company
lay bets with the barmen, who
unharmed by justified obeisance
display a natural humility.

The women, well, the women,
wear too much make-up or none,
according to age; tomorrow
is not vital enough, today is thorough.

And snakes who are not snakes
play ball in the gutter at closing time,
a sad and recurrent futility.

Up to a Point, Old Couple

Dipsomaniacs and necrophiliacs
danced in the twilight,
while three wise photophobes
sat with their backs to the window.

Great cities are witches, one said,
they make you dance to their tune,
every city has a different tune.

The great are great, said the second
They will kiss you if you love them.

The great are great, said the third,
they will love you if you kiss them.

Paris is the only city in the world,
said the first,
you can be a dandy or have a black mistress.
Nobody cares.

Spinsters who are always middle-aged
sit on benches in the park,
said the third;
It's better to be a whore in a deck-chair,
said the second.

Talk is despicable
It sucks at the paps of your personality.

Poem

My songs are not spreading
their white wings on the boundless air
for the golden girls who staring
from office blocks know
that the clock in their heads
will stop at five and their lives
shall proceed whether joyful or dull
to the full capacity of their feeling;
they are stealing discreetly
to spring the soundless women
in cages whose dirges I sing
that they grieve for the caves
wherein lie their lost identities—lost
in their brothel-like hearts to those
who receive their love and believe
the touch-me trick of the quick
split-second conjuror
who glides his fingers up his sleeve
to produce the impossible dove.

1965 Thoughts to My Friends

We cry at the first impeccable
dawn of 1965,
Stay alive, oh, stay alive!
The last years took a heavy toll of friends,
their journeys' end; whose journey ends
as death, when you know it, seems despicable?

We love life, in the same way
that animals without surety
strange in their herds lose their disparity,
and battered in their life-love like MacBryde
we train our minds to the mornings and hide
our star that still shines and is dead
a million light-years away.

Now dawn, cold, calculating, hard,
you've made the grade once more
discarding the dross and guilt of '64,
the midnight bells rang on for lovers holding hands;
and ageing women clinging to their lands
and their brittle winter trees and howling dogs,
who threw on the fire another log
and clinked again the glasses,
knowing the white life is a lie that passes,
so believe no longer in the word;

so 1965 I dare you wake
up the dying numbers and tell them 'life'
perhaps in some warm corner of a pub at 4 o'clock
where shock is smoothed and less
than the grievous time that went
some other broken way and spent
each tawdry cash-drawn effort cached
in grief, itself, immoral, what else
offers the nervous system a tiny solace?
Come 1965 and give them a break!

For Brian Higgins, Died 9th December 1965

The news broke, It is a scandal
(dear God, how the family has dwindled.)
like brothers and sisters, we mourn
with mutual umbilical
this mathematician from Hull
who put off his calculus
to wear the poet's coat of dangerous cloth
and tread the merry and gregarious path
craving crumb from his inferiors.

He made a good job of it while singing
like Homer for his supper, bringing
a measure of gaiety to those
who suffered from his oneness of purpose.
He didn't opt out like Rimbaud.

With his hard sophisticated talent
what he had to say was left unfinished
and what he said was entirely relevant.

Dublin December 12th, 1965

She Was Rich

Chorus: It's the sime the ole world over
it's the rich what gets the blame
it's the poor what takes their lolly
isn't it a blooming shame?

She was rich but she was honest
though she came of doubtful stock
an honest heart was beating
underneath her Dior frock.

Heedless of her husband's warning
up to London she did go,
yearning for the seats of learning
in the pubs of dark Soho.

But the poor men saw this beauty
she knew not their base design
when they took her to an 'otel
and they charged her with the wine.

Then she took the poor men riding,
wreckers of rich women's souls,
and the devils did the steering,
in her 1920 Rolls.

Now they led her to an Hexclusive
Club de Caves de France,
and the 'Great' once so abusive
at her feet did sing and dance.

In the poets' arms she fluttered
as she called the rounds of drinks
Have them all on me she mutters
as the whiskeys too, she sinks.

But she'd soon spent all her money
and when she hinted with a cough
that she'd like a double brandy,
the 'Great' had wandered off.

Not a farthing had they left her
and when she wept they acted tough,
'We loved you as you was, love,
you was rich, but not rich enough.'

Standing on the bridge at midnight
she said Farewell blighted Love,
and they heard a splash, god help her
what is she a doing of?

See she sinks into the water,
with her chequebook she did part,
saying 'curse the useless object,
and damn the human heart.'

As they dragged her from the river
water from her clothes they wrang.
They all thought that she was drowned,
but the corpse got up and sang,

It's the same the whole world over
it's the rich what gets the blame,
that they don't stay rich forever,
isn't it a blooming shame?

… Take This Woman …

The sunshine kissed the church
and the bridegroom kissed the son
of the best man, who kissed the bride.

Inside the tabernacle
lay the body of our Lord,
and amongst the vestry papers
the proof of his loving word.

So to their carrot feast
went the two true vegetarians
(he much truer than she
who, not at all convinced,
would secretly rather far
have had champagne and caviar).

Now all the true vegetarians
gathered together to talk
(while the multiform numbers of Bach
in stereophonic sound
courted the dim background)
about the disastrous leather
the priest had around his feet
Condone the consumption of meat!

The wedding guests therefore looked
at the ravishingly beautiful bride
they, all joined by the registrar
couldn't believe the worst
that the traitor in their clan
had got married inside a church
The bridegroom did not subscribe
to the ridiculous Christian faith
so how did he wander off
on this dangerous thorny path?
Surely this was a case
of temporary aberration
where the study of Adler or Freud
might clear up the situation.

So the bride put down her veil,
put down her psalter too,
and then she said with a smile
that embraced the spartan room:
'You have forsworn your guilt
have scrubbed your bodies clear
and blameless may commit
the act of darkness at noon.
You have discovered for you
the only season for living
your eyes have seen the light
of a vegetarian heaven.'

And then she picked the glove
she had carelessly dropped on the floor
and said goodbye to her love
whom she might see no more.

But the wedding guests aghast
and amazed at what they'd seen
were hungry now for the feast
that would keep their bodies clean.
So they clapped the groom on the back
and said, 'You're a lucky man
to be rid of her so smartly
when she might have lingered on!'

Poem for Richard J. Riordan

If you only have tears
write a poem
If you only have laughter
write a poem

If you have no one to
put your arms around
write a poem
If politics condemn you
write a poem
If you can't pay your bills
write a poem

If there is no conspiracy left
write a poem
If you can't cure the doctors
write a poem
If literary sentences bore you
write a poem

If you have freedom to use and can't use it
write a poem

If you can't write another fucking poem—
burn the bucket.
And let out the canary

Dublin

Quote from daily newpaper, August 1968 ... "the root cause for this dreadful SCOURGE (alcoholism) was the fact that women treated their husbands as semi-detached relations."

Semi-detached or not
the Dubliner,
having no other habits
good or bad,
nevertheless
has drinking habits

The parish priest
worried about the alcoholism
of his parishioners
locks up his drink

The protestant clergyman
constantly worried
about this and that
especially the drinking habits
of his dwindling flock
and dashing madly
from one parishioner to another
visiting hospitals
amalgamating parishes
opening and shutting schools
jumble sales
fetes
buying free milk
freeing bought milk
crying over spilt milk
drives his parishioners
to further excesses
of drink

The atheist
lurking in his ivory tower
passionate in his negativity
denies everything
except drink

The poet
is in any case
an inveterate drunkard
by his very calling
if he has such a calling
(whatever a calling is)

And all the other peripheral artists
like actors
and solicitors
and lawyers
and doctors
and unmarried couples
notwithstanding homosexuals
of both sexes,
down and out louts
with lone doubts
and all the other
wicked people
knocking around
or even those
who are not knocking around
or not wicked but merely
dreadfully influenced
by the wickedness of others

simply

can't pass a pub
without going into it.

The psychiatrist
who is quite a nice guy
just like you and me,
takes one massive swig
from his Hennessy five star
before making out
his yearly report,
while somehow or other
he evades super-tax

and knows

That if the worst came to worst
and all his patients
were cured
that the working classes
(for whom the state will pay)

they

unable to buy food
will buy drink

and the unemployed
unable to eat
Will drink.

The Third Born

The son, the first-born took the trade
love-in-a-parcel all wrapped up
in tinsel string and glaze.
Then a daughter came all fair
a dove of peace: Paloma.

But she the third-born
is come by grey hurt
out of a tundra,
a white nothing: vast
without peace or love

A parent, dead, now fossilized
within, which sends out doubt
that was in the first place gift,
rough-cast with small gravel
and quicklime.

And as Fenice, has emerged
betrothed to Cliges will marry an uncle
And confound a generation
of deed, will back into thought
creep meticulous as death
and without mercy.

All Head Down

The Eagle sheds its claws to Medusa;
gifts, like the serpent gave.
We believe in Gorgons!
scimitar to hand . . .

DOWN ALL YOUR HEAD

Hair dragged, entrails into the dawn
out of fish and mammal
that tunnel through the waves

SAVE THE US FUND

The dying US
reduced in the brittle shallows
like shards of riffled thoughts.
And then again
and then again
Reductions like angels
crowd the air
like a light made dark
by migrant birds.

And now we creep under
—not sheets and blankets
not even blankets without sheets
but under the very bed itself
squeezing through cracks in the floorboards
into the pillow dust
of rafter and joist
plaster and lath
and laughing huddle
scared of the dead rook
in the empty house

YOUR HEAD IS DOWN
BUT
Your insurance policy is paid up
premium stamped

breathing mortgaged
aches and pains to the pawnbroker
6 ½ %
Wastage .... wastage
all wastage washed and ironed
folded to taste and salted
put away like night's thunder

Demolition squads regimented in line
with anti-breath serum
tested as before
in perfectly hygienic circumstances.

But the sun comes back like a lie
A torn lie worn out with the telling;
one shaft of heat
a spit through a roasted human
barbecued, too, in the telling

I can't wait for the stiff stick
that drives through brain and sinew
like a bolt thrown out of pique
and the outer skin removed
neatly shaved, trimmed, or glazed
Everything is arranged
not least the morphine;
syringe to the ready
air excluded
one sixth of a grain
I can't wait for the telling
for the lie is back in the sun

Will we talk, then, in the trapped sun
disjointed fragments of accusations?

Or be deceived by the sympathy of pain?

Stephen's Green

The Child
The lame duck
and the Sergeant

The child
bobbing
feinting
stalking

Hovered between
sadism
and adult
compassion
while trying to catch the duck

the duck
quacking
started up a cacophony
of quacking till not only the ducks
but the other strollers
and flyers
were given over
to animal curiosity

The sergeant
who wore twenty silver suns
upon his coat
now found food for thought
in this entertainment
and believe me
he was hungry

He made a coup de grâce
worthy of his cloth
with one long lawful arm
he beat the child
with the other saved the duck

The grass stood up and stretched
an in-bred tulip sighed
nature (being wonderful)
is able to restore

everything
except a person's pride
that's shattered
by the humanity
of the law

A Friend of All is a Friend in Need

I am not afraid of anything
except civil servants
ESB men and midwives

I am alive on the other hand
to the dangers of relatives
bus-conductors and health visitors

I am dead duck to policemen
other people's God and public
telephones

But on the whole
I have nerves of steel
and feel like Mrs Atlas
holding up the universe
while Charles is in the boozer

Don't get me wrong
It could be worse
I'm not a loser
just terrified of people

The Boy Who Wouldn’t

Ah poor me,
sitting around waiting
for someone to say, Hey ho
merry soul and sing a paen

what sort of soul is that
that sits around waiting?
Tedium, tedium
Penelopean
give you a pain

It must be a silly sort of soul
pretty soft
stuck somewhere
like an owl on a tree

Ah poor me, poor soul
wretched and lonely
why doesn't it get on with its business
like any sensible soul
city soul
and go home regularly for its tea?

It needn't be a night soul
stuck in a tree
with folded wings.

What was good enough for its father
should be good enough for it;
O father soul
makest me like thee
wised up and workaday
so everyone will say
There's a fine soul
that a father's not ashamed of
making the best of things.

Sources for the poems in periodicals and from Bardwell's papers

Poem Title	*Source*
Fable	*Arena* No 1 1963
Sentimental Journey	*Arena* No 1 1963
The End of the Party	*Arena* No 3 1964
Lament	*Arena* No 3 1964
At Another Birthday Party	*Arena* No 3 1964
A Prayer For All Young Girls	*Arena* No 3 1964
And A Nursery Rhyme For All Girls	*Arena* No 3 1964
Portrait	*Arena* No 3 1964
Housewives	*Poetry Ireland* No 3 1964
Summer 1964	*Arena* No 4 1965
Star	*Arena* No 4 1965
The Lady Knew More Than Most	*Arena* No 4 1965
Portrait of a Pub	*Arena* No 4 1965
The Will, *Or* An Old-Fashioned Irish Short Story	*Arena* No 4 1965
Up To A Point, Old Couple	*Arena* No 4 1965
Poem	*Arena* No 4 1965
For Brian Higgins, Died 9th December 1965	Found among Bardwell's papers
Childhood Reminder	*The Holy Door* 1965
1965 Thoughts To My Friends	*The Holy Door*1965
She Was Rich	*The Holy Door* 1966
Take This Woman	*The Holy Door* 1966
Reward to Finder	*Castle Poets 1966* and *The Lace Curtain* No 3
The Circle	found among Bardwell's papers
Trouble In The Flat Above, or Familiar Irish Short Story	found among Bardwell's papers
Poem for Richard J Riordan	found among Bardwell's papers
Question	Hayden Murphy's *Broadsheet* No. 4
Dublin	found among Bardwell's papers, dated 1968
The Third Born	Chapter 2 of the poetry series *The Book of Invasions* 1969 (Tara Telephone)
All Head Down	Hayden Murphy's *Broadsheet* No. 8
The Dead	*Aquarius* 4, 1971, a variant of 'The Violets Of The Poor' from *The Noise of Masonry Settling*
They'd Been at it for Weeks	*Aquarius* 4, 1971
Pisces	Hayden Murphy's *Broadsheet* No. 11, early 1970s
Stephen's Green	Hayden Murphy's *Broadsheet* No. 10, March 1971
A Friend of All is a Friend in Need	Hayden Murphy's *Broadsheet* No. 10, March 1971

Poem Title	*Source*
The Boy Who Wouldn't	Hayden Murphy's *Broadsheet* No. 13 December 1971
The Novelist	*The Dublin Magazine*, 1971
Motor Accident	*Capella*, early 1970s, a variant of 'Hell's Angels' from *The Fly and the Bedbug*
The Poet Contemplates Suicide	*The World*, No 26, New York, Jan 1973
The Dream & The Awakening	found among Bardwell's papers
From Leitrim to Baggot Street Hospital	Hayden Murphy's *Broadsheet*, 1974
Mountain Funeral	*The Gorey Detail*, 1975
Amanda Sheridan	found among Bardwell's papers
Timor Mortis	found among Bardwell's papers
She Laid Her Children At Her Father's Feet	found among Bardwell's papers
Country Idyll	*The Stony Thursday Book 5 1977-78*, Limerick, a variant of 'Suburban Idyll' from *The Fly and the Bedbug*
Childhood Memory	*Poetry Ireland* No 4
Poems in Mem Stevie Smith: Useless Ghost & Paradox of the Morning Rider	found among Bardwell's papers
Conversation	found among Bardwell's papers
Chauffeur	found among Bardwell's papers
Outside the Dispensary	found among Bardwell's papers
Fathers	found among Bardwell's papers
Marlene Dietrich	found among Bardwell's papers
Paris	found among Bardwell's papers
That House	found among Bardwell's papers
Cancer	found among Bardwell's papers
The Colour Orange	*An Evil Cradling*, Brian Keenan, 1992
Birth	found among Bardwell's papers
And Every Crocus Laid	found among Bardwell's papers
Life Behind	found among Bardwell's papers
River	found among Bardwell's papers and included in *Cyphers* 90
The Climb	found among Bardwell's papers
The Descent	found among Bardwell's papers
Long Distance Bus	found among Bardwell's papers
February	found among Bardwell's papers
Workshop in Mountjoy Prison: Women's Wing	*Force 10* #8
The Song of the Saw	found among Bardwell's papers, variant of 'The Cross Cut'
The Cross Cut	*Soho Square Six*, London: Bloomsbury, 1993
Raven	*Poetry Ireland Review*, No 93
Mrs Russell	found among Bardwell's papers
The Single Voice in the Night	found among Bardwell's papers
The Day I Knew	found among Bardwell's papers

Poem Title	*Source*
DNA	found among Bardwell's papers
Colours	found among Bardwell's papers
Council proposes €75 fine for breach of beach laws	*Force 10* #13 2008
Cloonagh Grows	found among Bardwell's papers
Islands	found among Bardwell's papers
Tears	*Cyphers* 65
Ugly as Sin	*Cyphers* 65
80 Year Old Lady	*Cyphers* 53
Snow	*Light Years*, 2007, produced by Eiléan Ní Chuilleanáin for Pearse Hutchinson's 80th birthday
The House That Jack Built	found among Bardwell's papers
Friends At The Rubbish Dump	found among Bardwell's papers
Crossing the Brow	*Cyphers* 71
Room	*The Cathach*, Sligo Library, 2011
Seven Rings	*The Cathach*, Sligo Library, 2011
My Belief In Summer	found among Bardwell's papers
The Dancer	found among Bardwell's papers
Mother Mer—Seal Sequence I—VI	found among Bardwell's papers No 2 was published in *The Cúirt Annual* 2006
Counties	found among Bardwell's papers and included in *Cyphers* 90
Pain	found among Bardwell's papers
No Tragedy	found among Bardwell's papers

Many poems in the published collections also appeared in periodicals such as *Poetry Ireland Review, Ambit, The Stony Thursday Book, Fortnight, Cyphers, Force 10* etc, but these references are not given here.

Index of Poem titles

PRAISE FOR LELAND BARDWELL'S POETRY

Dostoevsky's Grave

"Such sharpness, blended variously with feelings of anger, warmth, wit and painful but unselfpitying or affectionate but unsentimental memory, are characteristic of her best work here."

TOM HALPIN, *Poetry Ireland Review*

The White Beach

"This work is revolutionary. Its power derives in large measure from the combination of the real and the surreal; the outer shell and the inner workings of the human psyche."

JEAN DUNNE, *Irish University Review*

The Noise of Masonry Settling

"There is much wisdom in these pages and that—combined with the deft skill of a true poet— makes for great poetry."

SEAN WALSH, *Rambles.net*

The Fly and the Bedbug

"Her poems offer, along with often stinging pictures of society and the human beings at odds with it, shifting, sometimes brilliant imagery and rhythmic energy."

EILÉAN NÍ CHUILLEANÁIN, *Poetry Ireland Review*

salmonpoetry
Cliffs of Moher, County Clare, Ireland

"Publishing the finest Irish and international literature."
Michael D. Higgins, President of Ireland